Geoff Tristram was a professional ar[...] over 45 years, during which time he [...] of clients including Ravensburger Pu[...] Doulton, Embassy World Snooker, [...] Times, Winsor & Newton, Trivial P[...] show, 'They Think It's All Over', to name but a few.

He has painted or drawn celebrities including Jeremy Clarkson, Jonathan Ross, Sir Ian Botham, David Vine, Alan Shearer, Ian Hislop, Ken Doherty, and Gary Lineker, not to mention caricaturing virtually every snooker player from the 1980s and 1990s that you can mention.

Geoff has also designed many book-covers, advertisements, album sleeves for bands such as UB40, The Maisonettes and City Boy, and postage stamps, notably 'Charles and Diana – The Royal Wedding', 'Lake Placid Winter Olympics', 'Bermuda Miss World', and Spain's 'World Cup Football' editions. He was even asked to paint the 400th anniversary portrait of Shakespeare for Stratford-upon-Avon council – his proudest artistic moment! Meanwhile, his 'Cat Conundrum' puzzle paintings and his many Ravensburger jigsaw cartoons continue to delight, intrigue, amuse and baffle dedicated fans all over the world. Geoff's younger brother, David, is an internationally-known and extremely successful comedy playwright, so it was no real surprise that Geoff would also turn his hand to comedy writing, hence this, his fifth full-length novel to feature Adam Eve, the endearingly chaotic and obsessive writer, working alongside Geoff's other main character, artist David Day. And on that note, it states quite clearly in the disclaimer section on the publisher's information page that all characters in this book are completely fictional, and not based on persons either living or dead. Geoff would like to point out that any characteristics that the central characters of this book and its author might share are purely coincidental.

The Artist's Revenge

Geoff Tristram

DRAWING
ROOM

Printed and bound by 4edge Ltd

Contact the author on gt@geofftristram.co.uk

ISBN 978-1-3999-4934-7

Cover design by Geoff Tristram and Steve Jolliffe.

Time flies, doesn't it? Only ten minutes ago I was a naïve, innocent, artistic and gentle-natured nine-year-old Black Country boy having private clarinet lessons that my parents probably couldn't afford, and now, all of a sudden, I'm sixty-eight, I've morphed into a Phil Collins-lookalike, painted or drawn some 50,000 images for the advertising and publishing industries, and written 20 novels. A lot of my books were about a character called David Day, a scatterbrained and chaotic artist. The others were about Adam Eve, a scatterbrained and chaotic writer. I often wonder where my inspiration comes from. This latest offering is an Adam Eve *and* David Day novel.

I retired as a professional artist this year, and it was a strange, poignant time for me. All I've ever been is an artist and cartoonist. If you sliced my head off, you'd see the words 'Artist and Cartoonist' in a circle on my neck, like on a stick of rock. Please take my word for this and don't try it.

There are only so many times you can drive to Kidderminster, have a cup of tea with your wife in Marks & Spencer's café, and then browse around the store, or maybe around T.K. Maxx. It keeps her quiet, but to a man blessed, or maybe cursed with a super-creative comedic mind, it's like treading water and waiting to die. Suddenly I feel utterly worthless, so to combat this, I decided to attempt what could well be my final Adam Eve comedy, having done the same last year for my old friend, David Day. Actually, they were both together in a book entitled 'A Remarkable Chain of Events' not long ago, and *that* was a work of genius, so I thought I would include David in this one as well. They were a great double act, and this book is about Art, after all, so it works well.

It's very sad that I recently painted my last paid-for picture (until the next one) but at least now I have more time to write my comedies. That's if my ancient, tired old brain can still manage it. I'll let you be the judge of that! Thanks for your continued support,

love Geoff x

No matter how awful an experience is,
it will usually serve you well as an oft-repeated anecdote,
once the dust has settled.

CHAPTER 1
The Newspaper Article

My name is Adam Eve. I'm a writer, which always sounds grander than it is, at least in my case. I've written loads of articles for magazines, and mainly the free papers, and I've also written a handful of comedy novels, usually based on my own real-life experiences, which were then titivated to make them a bit funnier.

And before you ask, Adam Eve is my real name, not a pen-name. My late mother, bless her, was rubbish at naming her kids. She never thought it through. I don't think it even dawned on her that my name was a biblical joke, and my brother Steven and sister Evelyn didn't fare too well either, especially when they used the shortened form.

Come to think of it, Adam Sheaffer, or maybe Adam Parker would have been good pen names for me, I reckon, had I needed one, but enough of this frivolity, for now at least. My past exploits, that have been immortalised in my books, have involved missing pantomime horse's hoofs (yes, really!), rare Māori carvings, lost Shakespeare portraits, stolen manuscripts, psychopathic killers and so on; all great stories, I'm sure you'll agree, but this one involves a potential miscarriage of justice, a human tragedy, a lost masterpiece, and best of all, an intriguing set of hidden, cryptic clues. And it's funny as well!

It all began a year or so ago, one afternoon when I was bored, dare I say it, shitless. I had no paid work to do –

this job can be very sporadic – and no good ideas for a new novel. I was feeling as flat as the tyre on my twelve-year-old knacker of a car, so in desperation I picked up that day's copy of the Daily Mail to scan while I ate my morning toast, and spotted an article that *really* grabbed my attention.

An eccentric, elderly artist named Michael Waldron, who, coincidentally lived in my home town of Stourbridge, in the West Midlands, had committed suicide in one of the five Staffordshire prisons that litter the A449. I forget the name of it, but they have one for ladies, one for young men, one for paedophiles, one for general, run-of-the-mill naughty folks – you get the idea. He was in the general naughty folks one by the way, and serving a five-year sentence for stealing a very valuable Canaletto painting from a stately home, also in Staffordshire. All very tragic of course, but it was the next bit that intrigued me. Apparently, he had accused the Earl of Eggington, Lord Charles Billingham, of refusing to pay for a portrait that Michael had created of the 55-year-old earl's wife, a 35-year-old Anglo-Italian beauty by the name of Suzannah Tavola, who also came from a well-to-do family.

The earl insisted that he had never known or contacted the artist, whom he said turned up unannounced at the stately home – which was run by The Heritage Trust and therefore open to the public – ranting and rambling on incoherently about a sum of £15,000 that he said the earl owed him for the portrait. The earl said he had no knowledge whatsoever of any portrait, and categorically

2

denied commissioning it, adding that the eccentrically-dressed old artist had completely lost the plot and was clearly delusional. He duly rang the local police, who instructed the man to desist and disappear sharpish, unless he fancied being arrested. Even in the face of this, Michael continued to warn the earl that he would wreak his revenge. In the spirit of fairness, the police took a statement from Waldron, who told them that the earl had insisted that, along with handing over the finished portrait, he should also include the preliminary photographs, sketches and all preparatory work. He explained that he liked to collect the associated items for his archive, because he found the entire process interesting and informative. His ancestors had done likewise with John Singer Sargent, Poussin, Joshua Reynolds, Sisley and the others they had commissioned, back in the day, and now the hall had a wonderful collection, not only of masterpieces, but also of sketches showing how the finished paintings were created. The museum was, consequently, very popular with the visitors. Michael was flattered by this interest in his preparatory work, but now it meant that he didn't have a single piece of evidence to support his claims. He insisted that the earl had met him in a café to hand over the reference photo, and in a country lane when the finished artwork was handed over. The reason for the subterfuge was that the portrait was to be a surprise birthday present, so the earl didn't want Michael turning up at the hall with it and being spotted by Suzannah. He'd promised to get his secretary to send the artist a cheque the following day, but he never did.

3

Taking this on board, the police politely requested that they should be allowed to search the huge house for any evidence that the portrait existed, to which end they turned up with a search warrant and without warning, and this amused the earl no-end. Nevertheless, he allowed them free-rein of the building, the archives, the tied cottages and the mews, and stormed off to take it out on a few pheasants until they'd all left. Or maybe he said peasants.

They found nothing whatsoever, and having done their best to be fair to both parties, they gave up and went home, leaving Michael apoplectic with rage.

Then, the following week, the earl discovered that his £15,000,000 Canaletto painting, entitled, 'View of the Grand Canal', just like all the others, was noticeable only by its absence. All that was left was a slightly cleaner rectangle of flock-sprayed yellow wallpaper where it had once hung. He immediately called his security man, who studied the external CCTV cameras at the front entrance, and eventually found what he was looking for. It was a dull, non-eventful Monday morning, just as the doors were opening, and there were only three people queuing to get in. It was still early, after all. Most people began piling in an hour or so after that. He was dressed down, in an old mac and a pair of jeans, and his usually dishevelled hippy hairdo had been tied up and hidden under a hat, but there was no mistaking Michael Waldron, and he was holding a black A1 artist's portfolio. They next examined the yellow room CCTV, and to their horror, found it was not working, but at least they had what they needed; evidence that he had visited the hall. The door lady that

4

day was asked if she remembered the man and she did, because of the portfolio. She'd asked him why he had it, as all good, security-minded people do, and he unzipped it to show her. Inside was 'a very nice painting', she said, of a view from the Clent Hills. The gentleman explained that he didn't want to leave it in his car, on the hall car-park, just in case it was stolen. He was delivering the picture to a client right after he'd popped to look around the hall, and he told her that the picture was being sold for £8,000 so he couldn't afford to risk it. He also mentioned to her that he'd been due to give a talk to an art society in Tamworth one Friday evening, stopped to ask directions at a hairdresser's salon, and during the two minutes that that took, some kindly soul had stolen his car. The lady understood his caution, and allowed him to proceed. She remembered him leaving an hour later, with his portfolio, and she shouted after him, 'Hope the sale goes well, sir!' He thanked her and left.

Michael had gone walkabout, but was eventually tracked down by the police and taken in for questioning. He admitted that he *had* visited that day, and seized his moment, when the yellow-room attendant slipped away to the lavatory, to unleash his Posidrive, quickly unscrew the two mirror-plates that secured the Canaletto to the wall, and slip it into his portfolio. When the police demanded that he returned the painting or face five years in prison, Michael steadfastly refused, adding that right is right, and he was a man of principle. The earl owed him £15,000, and until it was paid, the Canaletto was being held to ransom.

Inevitably, it all ended up in court. The judge heard that Mr Waldron had deteriorated mentally in the past year, after a career spanning some forty-five years, due to the death of his beloved wife, Pamela. He had once been a top-flight painter, commissioned by various celebrities, politicians and the wealthy country set, but in recent years he had spent a fortune on care homes for his stricken wife, sold his house and moved to a run-down flat, and generally 'let himself go'. That said, whilst the judge had considerable sympathy for his predicament, he couldn't allow people to waltz into stately homes and steal Canalettos. After hearing evidence from all parties, he also dismissed the artist's claim of being owed £15,000 by the earl as fantasy. He then turned to face Michael Waldron and offered him a deal. Return the Canaletto unscathed and he would receive a suspended sentence, as he had never committed any kind of crime before. Either that, or he would get five years, starting in ten minutes' time. Even then, the judge was lenient. He added that, should Michael find it within himself to reveal the whereabouts of the painting, he would be let out of jail. If he remained intransigent and pig-headed, he would do the full term.

Then, according to the very detailed newspaper report, which had me in its spell from the first word to the last, Michael informed the judge that he was a man of principle, and he was going to jail. Sadly, the story didn't end there. It got much, much worse. The police searched his neglected flat, and many other places where he might just have hidden the masterpiece. Nothing was found. Then, after a year had gone by, a warden called on

6

Michael one morning, worried that he had seemed in a very strange mood the day before, and was speaking gibberish. As he opened the cell door he was confronted by an awful sight. Michael Waldron had slashed his wrists and died. There was blood everywhere, and he was slumped over his bunk bed. On the wall opposite, he had written, with a finger dipped in his own blood, the following words.

Iron my clothes, Suzannah Tavama

Chapter 2
Eggington Hall

No one at the Staffordshire prison had any inkling as to what his final sentence meant. They presumed it was just part of his delirium. The psychiatrists put it down to the double trauma of losing his wife, and the peculiar Eggington Hall Affair, which he seemed to have conjured up from his imagination, as his befuddled mind deteriorated. Meanwhile, I was utterly transfixed by it all. I couldn't stop thinking about it. I know it sounds conceited, but I vowed to try and solve this bizarre conundrum, having done quite well with other strange incidents in the past. After all, I had nothing else to do. I suppose the fact that this man was a Stourbridge man, like me, drew me to it. I'd spent restless nights, tossing and turning, trying to fathom out what his last tragic, incoherent sentence, written in his own blood, seconds before he died, could actually mean, if indeed it meant anything.

I started to do some digging. Me, the Poundland Poirot, the Stourbridge Sherlock. Fat chance I had of unearthing anything, but I wanted to try. The first thing I wrote in my newly-acquired-for-the-purpose little notepad was that Michael had actually misspelt Suzannah's name. I put that down to nothing more than his confused state. I also found out where he lived, but for the time being, I could do nothing about that, as I wasn't thrilled at the thought of being arrested for breaking and entering. Instead, I asked around the estate, and was lucky enough to bump into a few old friends and neighbours of Michael's, and encouragingly, they all concurred. He was a nice enough chap, he dressed a bit like an ageing hippy, and his life had been turned upside down when his wife had a string of serious illnesses that forced him to place her in a care home, so she could be looked after properly. He would paint away in solitude, never letting anyone into his studio, and only ever leave to visit her or pop to the convenience store. Very occasionally, he would turn up at the local pub, sit on his own, nursing a pint, and then sidle off quietly into the night. If he ever ate a proper meal, they didn't know when it happened. He couldn't cook to save his life, and he appeared to be living on junk and fish and chip-shop fodder. His flat had peeling paint on the front door, and their brief glances into his hallway revealed a shabby interior. I thanked them profusely and returned home. I wrote in my new notebook.

Try to locate some of Michael's artwork

Visit Eggington Hall

Pop to see David Day

Ponder the message in blood

I drove out to the earl's place, once I'd raked up enough money to buy a new tyre. It cost me £150. I couldn't believe it! It cost me as much as the car did. Eggington Hall, Staffordshire, is a listed building, and has been run by the Heritage Trust for some time, but it was still the

9

home of Charles, 9th Earl of Eggington. He and his wife also had another house, apparently, and flitted betwixt the hall and their other place as and when required. The Canaletto was a fairly major factor in helping raise the visitor numbers, so the earl and the Heritage Trust desperately needed it back. As we know, Michael had been absolutely unwilling to co-operate, which infuriated the earl more than somewhat. He was still having to fight off weasel reporters who were firing impertinent questions at him about the portrait of Suzannah, which didn't help to calm his temper.

I paid my entry fee and headed straight for the yellow room, which was where the Canaletto was once situated. It was in the right-hand corner by the old grand piano. Now, there was just a gap, either side of which was a huge Caravaggio, a Titian, a John Singer Sargent and an impressionist painting of geese scooting over a lake at twilight, by Alfred Sisley. Elsewhere in the gigantic room were pictures by Van Dyck, Joshua Reynolds, Poussin – in all I added up around £160,000,000 of artwork, and yes, you did read that correctly. Even more if they ever got Canaletto back. The room also housed Roman-style busts, ornate chairs, a wall of leather-bound books and the obligatory suit of armour. Apparently, according to the flyer, it was also where they filmed the odd TV drama, which, along with the visitors, helped to pay for the upkeep of the place.

I chatted to the on-duty Heritage Trust lady, who was sat on an uncomfortable-looking chair by the door. I asked her if she'd met the earl and his wife, and she said she had, many times. The countess was lovely, she said, but, she added with a conspiratorial whisper, *he* could be a bit abrupt.

'I always had to call him Your Lordship, but his wife was totally informal. I didn't even have to call her Suzannah, let alone countess. Sue was fine by her. No airs and graces.'

'And what was her surname?' I asked. 'The chap who stole your Canaletto wrote her name in blood on his cell wall, but didn't he get her name wrong?'

The Heritage Trust lady shuddered visibly. 'Yes, horrible,' she replied. 'She is Suzannah Tavola and he spelt it incorrectly. I think it means Table in Italian; funny surname, Suzannah Table! Her mother and father lived in Italy and she came to England as a university lecturer, and stayed after she met the earl at a posh ball. They got married; it was his second marriage – the first one divorced him – so she took on his surname but she kept her Italian surname too, so officially she is Suzannah Billingham-Tavola, Countess of Eggington. Quite well off, I think, her folks were. I don't know if you know this, but this hall is used as a film set and also a posh wedding and events venue. Bits of "The Crown", "Downton Abbey", "Jeeves and Wooster", "Pride and Prejudice", "Persuasion", "Bridgerton", and several more were filmed here. Suzannah was left a beautiful house by her mother, on a tiny Island in Lake Maggiore, and they flit from here to there, depending on what's happening at the hall. There are three of them in total – not mothers, I meant islands of course – and they're known as the Borromean Islands I think, near to the town of Stresa on the edge of the lake. There's Isola Madre, Isola Pescatore, and her place is on Isola Bella, which means beautiful island. Alright for some, eh?'

'Yes,' I replied, 'I live on a small island as well, when I'm not in my 1930's semi in Stourbridge. It's the traffic island in Wollaston, by Aldi. So, you say it was actually Sue Tavola, and he wrote Tavama didn't he?'

And then it hit me like a sledgehammer to the brow. Sue Tavama. Suit of armour. Surely this was not accidental, surely, surely. And then it hit me again, but this time even harder. Iron my clothes. Iron, my clothes. My clothes are made of iron!

'Can I just open the visor on that suit of armour over there?' I asked. 'I'd love to look inside one of those things, for reasons best known to myself!'

'Oh no, I'm sorry!' she replied, 'you're not allowed to touch anything in here.'

'Not even if it leads to the Canaletto being found?' I asked, as I strode purposefully towards the suit of armour. She called after me, but I ignored her. I yanked open the visor, which, in my humble opinion, needed a squirt of WD40 – or UB40, as my ex-mother-in-law always called it – and peered inside. I could hear the lady getting out of her squeaky chair and stomping towards me. There was a piece of paper sellotaped to the inside of the helmet, which I quickly snatched, hopefully unseen, before closing the visor again. She was halfway across the room now, and gaining momentum, so I quickly opened the door, skidded across the parquet-covered entrance hall, through the front doors and ran to my car. I'd parked it a good distance away in order to avoid any CCTV cameras, and I hoped against hope that the one reported to be not working in the yellow room was still not working. If I did get a visit from the law, I would tell all, and add that I was working in the hall's interests, a bit like a private detective. I'd cross that bridge when I came to it. My adrenalin was pumping as I screeched off the gravel and down the 'A' road to freedom. I felt like James Bond and Jason Bourne rolled into one, and I allowed myself a cheeky grin in the rear-view mirror as my pulse and heart-rate gradually settled.

When I got home, I grabbed the folded sheet of paper, rushed into my house, flopped into my favourite armchair and studied it. I expected it to state where the Canaletto was hidden, but I was wrong. It was another cryptic note. How many of these bloody things was I going to have to solve to find the painting? Three, maybe, or five, or two hundred? It was best not to dwell on that. The note read;

**Ask his Grace where the Canaletto went.
He'll be stumped, no doubt!**

It was at this point that I resolved to call on my old friend, David Day. Not only was he a brilliant artist and picture restorer, but he had the kind of mind that could create riddles such as this, whereas I just become befuddled. Whether he could solve them too was a different matter, but it was worth a try. Besides, two heads were always better than one, and for all I knew, we might discover a load more of these bloody cryptic notes – a never-ending trail. I got lucky with Suit of Armour, but the story could have ended there and then if I didn't get help. I grabbed a bag of crisps to sustain me till lunchtime, jumped in the car and headed for Kinver.

Chapter 3
David Day to the Rescue

'Bloody hell!' said David as he opened the front door of his splendid barn conversion. 'Adam Eve, the brother I never wanted!'

It is worth explaining, at this juncture, who this friend of mine was, and why I knew him. A few years previously, our paths crossed when a nutty old professor from Stratford-upon-Avon convinced us that he was onto something of earth-shattering importance, and to cut a long story short, it was all about Elizabethan letters and a lost portrait of William Shakespeare. You'd be better off just parting with £8.99 and buying my book, to be honest. It's a killer story, and all true. Anyway, we went through a roller-coaster ride of an adventure, with paintings being stolen – yes, more of them; it's a recurring theme in my life – and after all that, we became firm friends and part-time adventurers. David is an artistic genius, if a tad sarcastic, with a hell of a sharp brain, and he was also a world-renowned picture restorer, who'd worked for all the major art galleries before he'd recently decided to call it a day. He was used to working on damaged Da Vincis, mangled Monets, wrecked Rembrandts; you name it, but like me, he seemed to attract chaos without trying. He has solved more crimes than your average copper, because he can't resist delving deeper into things. In another world, we could have set up a private investigations company and done well, I'm sure of it. Philip Marlowe and Sam Spade. Poirot and Holmes. We could have been called Day and Eve. That's quite clever and catchy, come to

15

think of it! I'd read in the local rags recently that he'd helped a Birmingham C.I.D. inspector to nail a psychopathic killer whose trademark was stuffing tea bags into his victims' mouths and then sealing them up with gaffer tape. Well, they all have to have a gimmick nowadays don't they? I blame the Hannibal Lecter books. The policeman didn't have a clue why the killer did this tea bag thing, but David studied the evidence, and the psychology of this individual, and worked out that he had something called 'Intermittent Explosive Disorder', which meant he'd go into a completely disproportionate rage over silly, trivial things, and consequently, he killed several local radio presenters for mispronouncing words, or using bad grammar! For example, he was livid about people who employed the irritating 'glottal stop', which is when people, for example, leave out the letter 'T', as in 'Li-oo' and 'Ci-ee', instead of saying 'Little' and 'City'. The killer stuffed the tea in their mouths to make up for all the missing 'T's. David Day is a genius! How on earth did he deduce that? His mind is not wired like normal people's, I swear.

'David!' I beamed. 'I've missed you!' I was truly delighted to see his daft face again after a couple of years absence. He invited me in. I said hello to his wife, Suzanne, as opposed to Suzannah – yes, I know it's confusing but concentrate – and somehow, he convinced her to make us a pot of tea, when it would have been just as easy for him to do it.

16

'And to what do I owe this royal visit?' he asked. 'I presume it's some crazy, complex plot you want me to become embroiled in, just to keep you company.'

'Erm, yes,' I grinned, and explained the Canaletto Conundrum, as I had christened it, in some detail. He was all ears, but not in the same way that, say, Gary Lineker is. I mean, of course, that he was fascinated by every word of it, as I'd hoped he would be. Remarkably, he had once known Michael Waldron. They were at art college together, back in 1970, in Wolverhampton, when it was reputed to be the best college of art outside of London. He was full of praise for Waldron's work, even magnanimously admitting that the chap was almost as good as he was. He remembered him as a bit of a far-out hippy type, a little insular, but perfectly friendly. David preferred to be a brilliant artist who didn't particularly look like one, rather than someone who deliberately tried to look the part. He found that the businessmen and women he had to deal with respected him more that way, whereas their attitude towards freakishly dressed, purple-ponytailed chaps smoking weed, covered in awful tattoos and calling everyone 'man' was far more condescending. He'd heard through the grapevine that Waldron had specialised in painting fine-art private commissions for well-to-do clients after leaving college, but he'd not been in contact with him for many years.

David, like me, had been extremely bored of late, now that his career was pretty much over and full-time retirement beckoned. He too was looking for an adventure, and now, it seemed, he had found one that was worthy of him. I showed him the note that I'd extricated from the jaws of the medieval knight, and he studied it in silence for a good few minutes before handing it back to me.

'That's an easy one!' he grinned. 'My old cricket club, Enville.'

I stared at him with a look of reverence, surprise and disbelief, all rolled into one, if you can imagine that.

'But surely you can't have worked all that out in two minutes,' I said. 'The suit of armour one took me two days.'

'I struck lucky!' he replied. 'I'm not saying I could be that quick with any more of them. Look! His Grace isn't some ill-informed reference to the earl. You don't call earls "Your Grace" as far as I am aware. This Grace is W.G. Grace the famous cricketer, captain of England. Enville is only an amateur club nowadays, but the ground was considered to be the biggest and best in the world back in the day – better than Lord's. There was an article in the London Illustrated News in 1857 to that effect. Our place was two acres bigger than Lord's and it was in better nick. The reason for this is that the stately home where the ground is situated, Enville Hall, was once the home of Lord Stamford, a keen player himself, who built the pitch in 1821. His grandson, the Right Honourable George Harry Grey, a member of the M.C.C., took over in 1845, and made the pitch even better, and in 1870, W.G. Grace played for South England there, and by all accounts didn't play very well. He only scored 10 and 14. The clue in the note is "He'll be stumped", which of course is a cricket expression.'

'Bloody hell!' I gasped. 'You're even cleverer than I thought you were. But how does all that help with finding the next flipping clue?'

'Well, my guess is that it'll be in the clubhouse. There's a photograph of W.G. Grace in the bar, with a framed article about all the stuff I just told you. My money is on it being taped behind the frame. It's a good place to hide things and no one ever looks there. Otherwise, I haven't got a clue! Let's have a drive down there tomorrow. There'll be a Sunday game on so we can sit and watch that, pop to the bar, and have a nose. Do you like cricket?'

'Well, yes, but I never played it. I know *you* used to.'

'I did, but I'm sixty-eight now and I haven't played for ages. I still know folks there though. We'll have a nice afternoon, you'll love it!'

I couldn't wait for Sunday to arrive. I met David at the Enville Hall ground at 12.30pm. All the players were arriving with their huge kitbags, and several of them knew David from the old days. He had briefly played for their 2nd or 3rd teams, so he was hardly Ian Botham, but compared to me, he was. I'd never bowled, batted, fielded or even kept score – the hardest job of them all, by all accounts. I barely knew the rules, but I did like to sit and watch. It had a lovely, calming effect on me, I found, and it helped lower the blood pressure. I loved the sound of leather on willow, the dreamy afternoons in the English countryside, the hot air balloons floating over the ground, and the flask of tea. It was Heaven.

I wandered over to the clubhouse and into the bar, where I immediately spotted a cluster of framed photographs on the wall. I tried to look casual and nonchalant, unlike my nervy performance at Eggington Hall. I needn't have worried. The handful of people who were in the room couldn't have cared less. My heart skipped a beat as I approached the pictures, because I could already identify the portrait of W.G. Grace. That huge beard was a clue. A daft grin formed on my face as I imagined him being given out 'Beard Before Wicket'. I promised myself that I'd grow up one day but there were no signs of it as yet. I quickly glanced around the room, but no one had any interest in what I was up to. I casually lifted the frame away from the wall, and Eureka! There it was, clue number two. O joy! It was a small envelope this time, held in place by a couple of strips of masking tape. I yanked it free and immediately slipped it into my jacket pocket, to be studied later. It was hard to keep the smirk from my face. I popped over to the bar and ordered two celebratory halves of lager for us, which showed how chuffed I was. Ordinarily, I never, ever drink alcohol until the sun has gone down. I took them outside and looked for David. He was engrossed in conversation with a middle-aged cricketer, so I wandered over and handed him his drink.

'Ah, Adam,' he smiled, 'Ta! This is Richard Spratley; Spratters to his mates. Did you find what you were looking for?'

'Yes, thank you!' I beamed.

'Fantastic!' he replied, winking. 'Well done! Look, something's come up and I need to run it past you. Spratters here is the captain of the 3rd team today, and they're playing against Oldswinford 3^{rds}. They're all old gits like Rich and me, or else fourteen-year-olds. Rich has just informed me that two of his players have had a flat tyre on the M42 near Bromsgrove and they'll be late. Do you fancy a game?'

'Erm, I can't play,' I admitted.

'Neither can any of these buggers!' laughed David.

'No,' I said, panicking slightly now. 'I mean I literally can't play. Never picked up a bat, apart from on the beach at Weston-Super-Mare years ago with my little boy, can't bowl, don't know half the rules —'

'You'll be fine,' he assured me.'

'I won't' I assured him.

'You will!' David had a way of beating me into submission with his tongue. 'Spratters has got some spare kit we can borrow. You can stand miles away on the boundary, and odds-on, the ball won't even come near you, and even better if we're batting. We'll be numbers ten and eleven, and by then the two lads on the M42 will have arrived and they'll take over.'

21

'Erm, okay,' I said, 'you show me what to do then.'

We followed Richard into the changing rooms and he introduced us to the lads, who were all very nice. I did warn them about my complete lack of experience, but they didn't seem to care. I suppose it's not like snooker, where you're on your own. It's a team game where most of them stand around doing bugger-all anyway.

'The firsts are up their own arses,' said a chubby, ginger-haired chap with red cheeks, 'but we don't give a shit. We just have a laugh. That's what it's all about, mate!'

This put me at my ease. I quickly slipped into a set of Richard's spare whites. The trousers that were at least a foot too short for me and covered in grass stains. I did wonder if they'd previously belonged to Warwick Davis. Outside, the two captains tossed a coin, and the Oldswinford captain, Jon Stanier, an estate agent and old friend of David, won, and elected to bat. Richard Spratley sent us to our fielding positions, and I ended up about eight miles away from everyone, and a few inches from the boundary rope. My only companion was a horse in the adjacent field that I decided to christen 'Cartwright', after Hoss Cartwright, a character from the old TV series, Bonanza.

The game got underway, or at least, I presume it did. I wasn't really involved. The Oldswinford batsmen were bashing the ball all over the place, but it never went anywhere near me; not that I wanted it to, you understand.

I was so bored, I retrieved the envelope from my pocket –
I was too paranoid to leave it in the changing room – and
studied the latest cryptic clue with more than a touch of
excitement. It read:

Turn again, down the A449,
when you're there,
you'll see the sign.
Oh, what a Grey Day!

I'd just about digested it when I heard a commotion
coming from the centre of the pitch. A few players were
shouting and pointing. Then I saw a red blur, and felt a
terrible, excruciating pain in the centre of my brow, like
I'd been shot, and I don't remember anything after that.
Oblivion! I woke up slowly and in agony. My eyes were
completely out of focus, like I'd had one of my migraines.
I didn't have a clue where I was, but I was vaguely aware
of a crowd of white-clad people all bending over me. Jon
Stanier, or at least, someone that looked like an out-of-
focus version of him, was standing with his legs either
side of my chest, looking down at me with a worried face
and asking if I was okay. He asked me how many fingers
he was holding up. He later told me I'd said two hundred.
I was delirious, apparently.

It transpired that he had whacked a huge, would-be six.
I say would-be. If I hadn't been standing next to the rope,
the ball would have cleared it without bouncing and gone
for six. Instead, it hit me square in the brow doing around
eighty miles per hour. It's a wonder it didn't kill me. My

23

first bit of cricket action, and I was busy reading a letter. While the lads gathered round with concern etched on their faces, David seemed to trying hard to stifle a giggling fit. He grabbed the letter, and read it. He didn't have a clue what it meant, and I no longer cared.

Chapter 4
Weird Dreams

I spent the next five hours at Russell's Hall Hospital being scanned, prodded and tested. At first, when I arrived, I was speaking in tongues and thought I was Napoleon Bonaparte. I had the Headache from Hell. The hospital doctor informed me that I was concussed. I could have told *him* that. Eventually, I improved a little, and they deemed me fit for release, with the proviso that I rang my local doctor's surgery right away if I felt ill. I hoped that wouldn't be necessary, as I was always 137th in the queue at the Lion Health Centre, my local place. I would often sit with the phone next to me for hours, listening impatiently with the aid of the speaker-phone thingy, as I slowly got nearer to speaking to a real human being, only for the phone to mysteriously cut off when it got to 3rd in the queue. I was not properly *compos mentis* for two or three days, and I experienced some weird dreams too. On the first night, I dreamt that singer, George Ezra, was sat on a red leather chair that was bolted sideways onto the side wall of my house, around twenty-feet up, and he was trying to play an electric piano that was also bolted sideways on (even though he plays guitar, not piano, as far as I know). His legs were around fifteen feet long, but he still couldn't quite reach the two brass pedals that were at floor level. He was begging me to help him. The next night I dreamt that there was an old-fashioned tin bath in my living room by the fire, and inside it was a large group of guinea pigs, all dressed in clerical dog collars, and they were all praying and making cute guinea pig noises. Their little paws were clasped together as they prayed. It was very moving, I thought. One thing was certain. I wouldn't be playing cricket again any time soon.

David, bless him, had arranged for my car to be delivered back to the house in my absence, and after taking a few days off to recuperate, I was eager to make up for lost time and tackle the latest clue. David had read it, pondered, and was confident that, once more, he was on the right lines. He remembered that 'Turn Again' was a phrase used in the story of Dick Whittington, the three-times Mayor of London, back in the day. That man was clever, I had to admit. David, I mean, not Dick, though he probably was too. The rest of the clue seemed to back up his theory. The A449 was a local road that went for miles in both directions, all the way from Stafford to Kidderminster, Worcester and probably way beyond that. However, the area Michael Waldron was referring to was just down the road from Enville, near David's barn in Kinver. It was the site of a famous old building that was built by Dick Whittington's grandfather, back in 1310. Nowadays it's a restaurant called the Manor House at Whittington, and before that, it was The Whittington Inn. The last part of the riddle mentioned the colour, Grey. This was a reference to Lady Jane Grey, later known as Lady Jane Dudley, the Nine-Days' Queen, who was tried for treason and executed at the Tower of London whilst still a teenager; a truly awful bit of English history. Apparently, according to David, who seems to know virtually everything, she once lived at the house, many years after the first famous family lived there. David presumed the bit about the sign was a reference to the pub sign, on the grass verge near the car park. We couldn't wait to find out, and to this end he picked me up in his lovely red BMW, which was a real treat compared to my clapped-out rusty Nissan Micra with one posh tyre. We swung into the car park, parked up, and I ran over to the sign, my excitement brimming over, like a kid on Christmas morning. I went over it with a fine-toothed comb, getting more and more exasperated with every second, and just as I feared that all was lost, there it was, in a plastic food bag to protect it from the elements, wedged into a gap where the top moulding of the sign's frame met the side moulding, and had slightly separated due to weathering. I screamed with joy, causing an elderly couple who had just arrived for lunch to quickly close the doors of their car again and wait, cowering within, until I'd gone. I got in the car, slammed the door shut and handed it to David. He feverishly opened the bag and unfolded the paper, and then put on his studious face as he digested the information. Finally, he turned to me with a puzzled look and confessed that he didn't have the foggiest idea what it meant. It said:

Stanley Baldwin,
Rudyard Kipling,
Charles De Gaulle,
211 frogs.
This one's a rib-tickler!
1633

'I think the old bugger must have gone mad just before he wrote this one,' sighed David. The others were not too bad, but this is off the scale.'

I can't tell you how disappointed I was. The clue was a closed book to me too. it meant absolutely nothing. I vowed to do some homework that evening, trawling through Google and looking for leads. David was going to do likewise, he said.

Something rather obvious finally dawned on me that day. David and I were the only people on the planet who could pursue this now. No one else was in the race. We had the first few clues, so they could no longer compete with us. If *we* didn't solve the puzzle, no one ever could. Michael's quest was now in our hands, and for his sake, we had to see it through, no matter how infuriating it became. For all we knew, he had really lost the plot and imagined this portrait of Suzannah, and the earl was the aggrieved one. Whichever party was in the right, it was our job to settle it. It was our responsibility to find the missing Canaletto, for art's sake, let alone Michael's, the earl's or the Heritage Trust's. It was also our job to find the missing portrait of Suzannah, if indeed there was one. Personally, I kind of hoped Michael was telling the truth and it was the earl that was a liar. He'd lost his wife, lost his mind, maybe lost £15,000; lost his life. He needed a champion now, to fight his corner. Thank God I had a partner who was equal to this. It was the challenge of a lifetime, but we'd only just begun, and already, we had stumbled at the fourth hurdle, with Lord knows how many more to go.

David dropped me back home. I took two soluble paracetamol tablets, microwaved some inedible crap, and turned on my laptop. This wasn't going to beat me.

Chapter 5
Stanley Baldwin & Chums

The first thing I typed into Google was Stanley Baldwin.
It told me he was the Prime Minister of the UK on three
occasions, his final time being just before World War 2,
when Chamberlain took over, and then, shortly
afterwards, Churchill. He was born – and here's the bit
that surprised me – just down the road in Bewdley, and he
was the Bewdley M.P. before becoming the P.M. from
Bewdley, so maybe Michael Waldron was asking us to
visit his family home, but what on earth had Rudyard
Kipling, Charles de Gaulle and a couple of hundred frogs
got to do with it? De Gaulle was French of course, so were
the 211 frogs *actual* frogs, like the sort de Gaulle probably
had on his sandwiches, or was this Michael Waldron
being a bit naughty and slightly racist?

I typed in 'Charles de Gaulle' and got a pile of stuff
about him being the President of France, and all that, but
nothing that linked him with Baldwin, so I tried Rudyard
Kipling, and likewise, I found loads of stuff about his
literary career, the Indian connections, 'The Jungle
Book', the poem 'If', and the fact that he died in 1936, but
nothing linking him to the other two. This was very
frustrating, and I could see all our hard work coming to
nothing if I couldn't come up with a connection. I moved
onto the bit about being a rib-tickler, and again, I couldn't
get anywhere with that. It just means a funny thing,
something that tickles one's ribs; a weird expression from
another era, but it added nothing to the debate. The date,
phone number, PIN number, or whatever it was, of 1633,

was likewise not contributing to the sum-total of my knowledge, so I made a cup of tea and took deep breaths to calm myself down a bit. I tried again. This time I had a breakthrough. Rudyard was named after a Staffordshire lake – never heard of it! – that his mom and dad visited one day, so a local connection at last, but then I found the *real* connection. Old Rudyard and Stanley Baldwin were actually cousins. Well I never! This was progress of sorts, but it still didn't take me any further forward. I looked up Baldwin's home in Bewdley; it was called Astley Hall, so maybe we had to drive there and see if anything made more sense. Then the doorbell chimed, so I sighed a heavy sigh, stood up and went to the front door, annoyed by the interruption. It was my neighbour, Anton, returning a book I'd lent him on Norman Rockwell, the great American illustrator. Neither of us were any good at art, unlike David, but we both appreciated it, and I had quite a lot of books on the subject. Anton asked what I was up to, and I explained that I was trying to find a connection between Baldwin, Kipling and Charles de Gaulle. I lied and said it had been a quiz question at The Red Lion pub that I frequent, and I'd gone home before we got the answers, so I was curious.

'Oh, I can tell you that!' smiled Anton. 'They all stayed at Ribbesford House during the war.'

'WHAT?' I asked, as nonchalantly as I could, which was not very, as you can see by the use of capitals. The RIB word instantly confirmed to me that at last I was on the right lines. A breakthrough!

'Ribbesford House, near Bewdley. Baldwin was the Prime Minister and Kipling was his cousin, and they often visited there for whatever reason. Apparently, later on when the war began, Charles de Gaulle also visited to see how his army was getting on with their training.'

'I've gone giddy,' I told him, clutching the doorframe for support. 'Carry on. What army? Surely they were back in France, fighting the Germans.'

'Yes, they were, but a couple of hundred of them were sent to Ribbesford for training by our lot. Like a special forces, S.A.S. kind of thing, I think.'

'Anton, I think I love you!' I grinned. This seemed to take him into deep and unfathomable waters. 'It's okay,' I quickly added, 'I've spent ages getting nowhere with this and you gave me the full answer, so thank you very much! Apart from all that, there was another part to the question. What did the number 1633 have to do with it?'

'I don't have a clue,' he replied. 'Sorry, mate, now you've lost me.'

He made his excuses and wandered off back to his house. I couldn't wait to ring David and tell him I'd cracked it, all by myself, well, sort of. Meanwhile, I looked up Ribbesford on Google maps, (that Google lot can do EVERYTHING!) I worked out how to get there, and an hour later, we were setting off down the beloved A449 to Wolverley, and then onwards to Bewdley in search of our next clue. It was a nice, sunny day, so we decided to park up at Bewdley, and walk to the place. I'd taken my walking boots just in case the paths were muddy, and David had forgotten to. He was wearing a fancy pair of very expensive, yellow-ochre-coloured brogues, which, I have to say, were totally unsuitable. The pair of us were very excited about it all, but I think we both shared a nagging doubt about if the mad clues would actually lead us to the Canaletto, or just string us along before telling us both to eff off. There was also the vexed question of how many cryptic clues there were to find. Might this adventure pall a little after the 75th clue was found, with still no end in sight? Then I began to focus on yet another aspect of the clue hunt.

'I've just had a thought!' I said, as we marched up a hill past a few Georgian houses, en-route to the woods.

'It had to happen eventually,' smiled David, who surely must have done a joint degree in art and sarcasm at Wolverhampton. I ignored it and ploughed on.

'This has been troubling me. Michael Waldron set up who knows how many of these clues, which he then delivered to their hiding places, seemingly all over the West-bloody-Midlands, so how come his *first* clue was delivered just before he tragically died, which must have been a year after the others were hidden. It doesn't make sense, does it?'

'Bloody hell, Adam, you're absolutely right,' said David, 'but what if he set up the 'Iron my clothes, Suzannah Tavama' one first, somewhere like maybe in his flat? Surely, that place must have been the first port of call for the police, and he expected it to progress from there, but it didn't. The first anyone heard about this clue thing was his bloodied scrawl on the cell wall, as you rightly say, a full year after the others were hidden. My guess is that whoever searched the flat didn't do a very thorough job and it was missed somehow, so to make sure, he *rewrote* it in blood. We really need to have a peek into that flat as soon as possible. You never know, we might even find a bit of reference material for the portrait of Suzannah that the cops missed. The problem is, how do we get inside the place without breaking and entering, and then getting ourselves into trouble? And is the place still full of his belongings after a year? When I get back, I'll contact Jon Stanier. He's an old mate of mine from the cricket days, as you know, and he and his wife are part of our pub-quiz team at The Plough, but he's also an estate agent. Maybe he can give us a few tips. Meanwhile — aaaaaaaarrgh!'

David's next sentence was dramatically interrupted by him sliding backwards down a steep grassy-cum-muddy slope we'd been climbing. He must have slithered around ten feet on his stomach before he ended up in a gorse bush. To make matters worse, he appeared to be trying to use his chin as a handbrake. It was around two minutes before he said anything, and then it was a rude word which I'd rather not repeat. I, of course, laughed so much it hurt, which prompted him to repeat the same word, only with 'off' at the end of it, which for some reason, only made me laugh more. I was reminded of his reaction when the cricket ball nearly took my head off – they are made of solid wood in case you weren't aware – so I felt entitled to laugh as much as I wanted. After all, I was badly concussed, and spent five hours in A & E, and all he had was a slightly-sore chin, and muddy clothing. It looked as if a cow with dysentery had shit all over him and then ran away. I graciously helped him to his feet, and told him he should have brought his walking boots. Those Church brogues were two hundred quid and had smooth leather bottoms. Hardly the right attire for a walking trip. However, I didn't rub it in, and we carried on towards Ribbesford village. Walkers going in the opposite direction would go past us and start tittering, which didn't lighten his mood.

Eventually, we entered the little village, which looked like a film set. We could see the grand old house in the distance, with its two distinctive turrets, but signs in the lane made it clear that trespassers were not tolerated. To our right was a beautiful old church, with a graveyard that circled it, and that, without getting told off, was pretty much as far as we could go, so we went in through the front gates, stroked a cute greyish-blue cat with yellow eyes who was sat on the grit bin, and had a look around. Maybe, we thought, there was a way around the woods at the back to get a better look at the house. We approached the front door of the place, which had a white wooden porch over it, with a lovely tiled floor. The stone surround to the ancient studded door was intricately carved, but it was the little plaque at the centre of the porch's apex that stood out for me. It was a sign that told us how old this beautiful church was. It was built in 1633.

David looked at me, and I looked back at him. He clutched my arm and smiled. We walked under the porch and scrutinised every bit of that woodwork. I reached up to the left-hand corner, where there was a small shelf built into the framework, and fumbled around. It took a few seconds to feel all along it, but nothing was there. I switched my attention to the right-hand side. I felt something immediately. Something plastic. I pulled it down and nearly wet myself with joy. It was another small envelope, just the same as the one at the Whittington Inn. The Dynamic Duo had done it again. I ripped the bag open, opened the envelope with hands that were actually trembling, and there was our next clue. It read:

Well done!
That was a hard one, wasn't it?
Now treat yourself.
Go and see a play.
Hamlet maybe.
To be, or not to be,
that is the question.

Chapter 6
Michael's Flat

We trudged back from Ribbesford, full of the joys of spring. Even David's filthy clothes couldn't subdue his cheery spirit. We were singing out loud as we met the mighty River Severn, much to the anger or else the amusement of the local anglers, depending on their temperament. We were just approaching the Bewdley by-pass bridge on a single-track riverside path, with around fifteen minutes to go before the car park, when David suddenly stopped singing halfway through 'Weather with You', by Crowded House, a band we both loved.

'Everywhere you go, you always take the waaaaaaaaay!' he sang, and I looked behind me to see why he had so drastically changed Neil Finn's lyrics, just as I heard a loud 'Bladooooosh!' noise. David had picked his way nervously down a particularly steep little section of muddy path and suddenly morphed into a slalom skier, only instead of gliding gracefully at speed down a Swiss mountain, his yellow-ochre Church brogues shot him straight into the River Severn before he could grab a passing tree branch. It was all over in a split second. Thank God the bit he went arse-first into was quite shallow, because it transpired that David had never learnt to swim. Again, instead of sympathy, I doubled up with laughter, and I was laughing so hard it *really* hurt this time. The more I tried to stop, the more I couldn't. I reached down and helped him out of the freezing cold water, and some git a few yards away called him a tosser because he'd frightened all the fish away. As if all this wasn't bad enough, he had to walk for another fifteen minutes in drenched clothing, shivering like a jellyfish, and then drive back to Stourbridge in his underpants, and wrapped in an old tartan shawl covered in cat hair that he'd found in his boot, to keep him warm and prevent him from soaking his lovely leather seats. He looked like a Poundland version of Rob Roy, and I had to avert my eyes all the way home for fear of it starting me off again. Those muddy yellow-ochre brogues and green and pink ankle-socks did *not* go with the rest of his outfit, I have to say. I must admit that he is great company though; always funny. Apparently, he does a codeword puzzle every morning while he and Suzanne sit in bed drinking tea. He reckons it sharpens his mind ready for the day ahead. He loves wordplay too, and often comes up with ridiculous similes such as, 'I'm as cold as a goldfish that's been in the fridge all night.' Total nonsense, but amusing. He also asks daft questions apropos of nothing, such as, 'If you had three pet crows, Adam, what would you call them?' I look at him nonplussed, and he says, 'I'd call mine Russell, Sheryl and Upstart'; the last one being an obscure Shakespeare joke apparently, so naturally, I said that I didn't get it, and he told me that the batteries were dead in my joke-detector. Then he asked, 'And what if you had a pet squirrel?' Apparently, he would call his squirrel 'Regis'. When I asked who or what Regis Squirrel was, he explained that it was supposed to be Squirrel Regis, the footballer, and I still didn't have a bloody clue what he was on about. I swear the man is not wired like us mere mortals, but that also explains why he can solve the cryptic clues we had been given. Mind you, he genuinely hates cryptic crosswords, which seems contradictory. If he reads 'Limbless hyena satisfies football legend' or 'Backwards shuffle into biscuit tin causes chaos', and similar tosh, he immediately screws the newspaper page into a ball and throws it into the pedal bin. Apparently, he much prefers 'Flightless Australian bird, three letters.' I agree that normal crosswords are better, apart from when they ask for the name of the actress who played the princess's grandmother in 'Game of Thrones', or 'Who scored the winning goal in the 1934 World Cup final?'

An hour later, he rang me to give me some good news. After he'd had a hot shower and put on some new clothes, he rang Jon Stanier, the cricketing, pub-quizzing estate agent who nearly took my head off, to ask him how one might enter a flat and have a nose around. Jon told him that he couldn't be a part of that kind of thing, for obvious reasons, but asked where the property was that David had an interest in. David gave him the address, and apparently Jon nearly choked on his cup of tea. This weird story was full of unlikely coincidences. It transpired that he had been asked to sell the place for the estate only a few days previously, and also to arrange the disposal of the contents. He was due to visit it to see what state the flat was in, and what was there in the way of belongings, furniture and so on, and David's call could not have come at a better time. Michael Waldron, it emerged, did have one distant relative, who had been contacted. The lady was thrilled to have been left a flat, but didn't want the contents, which was just as well, as Michael had written a will which dealt with all of that. He wanted any of his possessions, paintings and furniture that his relative didn't want, to be sold at auction to raise money for the Cobden

Hospice, where his wife had been looked after. Anything else of no importance could be chucked onto a skip. Michael had also asked William the solicitor to chuck him on a skip too, when he'd shuffled off his mortal coil, but the solicitor had persuaded him to allocate a sum to cover his funeral instead. Jon was due to visit the flat the following day, and asked if David and Adam wanted to come with him, for 'a viewing'.

As the three men entered the premises the first things they saw in the tiny hallway that led into the living room were: on the right, a weird, garish typographical painting, and on the left, an old gilded mirror that had seen better days. Three full-grown men in that particular hallway felt like two too many, so Jon and I proceeded into the living room, leaving David to study the garish artwork, which was not at all the kind of thing that Michael Waldron was noted for. It was more like a piece of ghastly pop art done by a student in a rush. All the letters were from different fonts, and in different colours and sizes, for a start. It read:

YM NORi
SEhTOLC
HANNAZUS
AMAVAT

At first, David guessed that it might be Latin or Greek; an old proverb maybe. Then he happened to spot its reflection in the old mirror, opposite, and at first, it was no clearer, thanks to the jumble of sizes and typefaces, but then he got it. Another Eureka moment in a story full of them. It was Michael's first-ever clue written backwards, just to make it even more indecipherable, as if it wasn't obscure enough to begin with. 'Iron My Clothes, Suzannah Tavama'. The original, no-blood version. He burst into the living room, fists raised high in triumph, and announced that Clue No.1 was indeed in the building, as he'd suspected it might be. Jon was busying himself going from room to room, jotting down what was available for auction or charity shop, and I was ferreting around in old carboard boxes, removing bits of paper and old receipts that looked potentially relevant. I leapt to my feet and followed him into the hall, where he explained it to me. It was a thrilling moment, I have to say. I then asked him to look at what *I'd* found. Not quite as dramatic, but equally satisfying. There were two receipts and two invoices stapled together that interested me. One was for a gilded picture frame from a company called Frinton's Frames, of Frinton on Sea. David immediately recognised this, as he also used the company. They made high-end frames for good quality paintings. Expensive, bespoke, and classy, he told me. Not your common High Street mouldings. You only bought these for posher houses and stately home-style heritage stuff. The swept frame was for a twenty by thirty-inch oil painting, he explained. I asked what 'swept' meant, and he said it was the twiddly stuff at the corners and the middle. Not cheap at £300, but all hand-made, with an off-white slip. That's the inner bit that meets the canvas, he added. Stapled to the invoice was another one, from a company called Dunn's in nearby Cradley Heath. David knew this firm too. They were a professional photo lab. The invoice stated 'colour photograph enlargement on matt paper from artist's camera', and also stapled to the invoice was a receipt and a sheet of notepaper with a hand-written instruction which read:

Paul — take image from Nikon.
Enlarge to 30 by 20 inches.
Client's email and scanner are down, so
can't send attachments.

This was very interesting to David. The proportions, the posh frame, the enlargement, they all suggested a portrait. He asked Adam if he'd spotted a Nikon anywhere. He hadn't, but a quick search produced a dusty Nikon D40 in Michael's computer table drawer, and also a key-ring with just one key on it, and a tatty old key-fob with the words THE ARTIST written on it in Biro. I know it was naughty, and Jon would have told me off, but I pocketed it, just in case it was of importance to our investigation. David switched the camera on, but alas, it did not respond. He rummaged around for a while and produced the Nikon battery charger. He slipped the battery out from under the camera and fitted it into the charger, which he then plugged into the nearest plug socket. This would take some time, he said, so meanwhile, we had another look around the place. It was run-down and scruffy, but some of the paintings on the walls, or propped up in spare rooms and in his studio, were exquisitely done. Even David said they were, and he's fussy. They would hopefully fetch a lot of money for the hospice, and David told me he'd be bidding for one himself, as a keepsake, and a sad reminder of this weird and tragic story. I would have loved one too, but I don't earn the kind of money that he did.

I went back to my old boxes to see if there was anything else of interest, and I spotted a theatre ticket for the Royal Shakespeare Company in Stratford, from the year before Michael Waldron ended up in jail. It was randomly pinned to the wall and someone, presumably Michael, had drawn a circle around the seat number in red pen to draw attention to it. I called David over to take a look, and I'm glad I did. What we had found was surely the inspiration for Waldron's latest clue. He'd been to see Hamlet, which was David's favourite Shakespeare play. He'd loved it since grammar school, and could still quote huge chunks of it fifty years later. In 2016, David had been asked by Stratford-upon-Avon's town council to create the official 400th Anniversary portrait of the Bard, something that made him extremely proud, and during that period he had been flitting to and from the town all the time, liaising with the mayor, the town clerk and others, keeping them abreast of his progress. The picture took him ten gruelling weeks to complete, and they were very pleased with the end result. His artwork was shown in the national press, and the local Stratford papers and magazines. It was also shown on the BBC and ITV channels, which thrilled his elderly mother no end. Now, Waldron's clues seemed to be pointing us in the direction of Stratford. The latest clue was wonderfully vague. Treat yourself, go and see a play,

Hamlet maybe. To be or not to be. But how on earth could they know where his latest clue was hidden from that? Maybe it was somewhere at the theatre, but where?

David took the ticket stub from me and stared at it intensely for ages. I thought he might be about to have a soliloquy. I looked around for a skull for him to hold in his other hand but I couldn't find one, other than the bruised one that was still in my head, and he wasn't having that until I'd finished with it.

Then, all of a sudden, he yelled 'YES! Got it!' The clue is hidden in an RSC theatre seat. It's Row B, seat 2.'

'How can you know that?' I asked, flabbergasted.

'Because, look, this ticket is for that seat. Right close to the front on the left-hand side. 2B or not 2B? That is the question. Well, this is row B, seat 2. It must have amused him, because it's 2B, and he's there watching Hamlet!'

'Bloody hell!' I gasped. 'Bloody hell! You really are the reincarnation of Sherlock Holmes, aren't you? So did he go to the theatre before the clues were being hidden and go back again to plant it or what?'

'Lord knows, but I bet you any money that's where it is. Under the seat, or down the back of it, or whatever. We need to go to Stratford tomorrow and sort it.'

'But how will we get in? I bet they'll get shirty and refuse us entry. I only got the clue from the suit of armour by luck. That woman was coming to eject me. It'll be ten times harder to get in there, David.'

'It won't,' he replied. 'Leave that bit to me.'

Jon Stanier returned to the living room and asked how we'd got on. We told him the good news. All we now needed to do was to see if the Nikon had charged up sufficiently to be able to examine what pictures were in it. It had. David took control, as he had the exact same camera at home. He turned it on and scrolled through it. There were shots of canal boats, countryside vistas, the usual stuff he expected to see on an artist's camera, and near the end, there it was. It was a shot taken from a printed photograph of a pretty, dark-haired lady, maybe in her thirties. She was sat in a chair, Mona Lisa-like, hands in exactly the same position as hers, with a wall in the background that had a picture on it. David could tell that this wasn't taken from life, but from another photograph, because he could see the edges of the original print in Michael Waldron's copy. He'd obviously been handed a smaller print to work from, and he needed to enlarge it to the actual size of his painting, so, presumably, rather than pester the earl, if it was indeed him, for another larger version, he simply retook the picture and handed it to Paul at Dunn's to enlarge. This now tallied with the Dunn's invoice, and also the Frinton's frame.

What we were looking at was convincing evidence that a portrait was indeed painted, and delivered, along with the original reference photographs, both large and small.

44

What the earl didn't bargain on, however, was the old Nikon and the copied picture hiding within it.

It looked very much like poor old Michael Waldron was telling the truth, but why was Lord Charles, Earl of Eggington, insisting that he'd never met the man, and not handing over his £15,000?

Things were hotting up! We locked up and left the flat. The next day, we were heading for Shakespeare country, and we couldn't wait.

Chapter 7
Stratford-upon-Avon

We set off in David's BMW at around 10 a.m. I did offer
to take him in my car, but he was worried that it might not
ever reach our destination. We took the M42, switched to
the M40 and got off at junction 16, so we could drive
through Henley-in-Arden, which was lovely. All those
conspiracy theory dick-heads who think Shakespeare
didn't write the plays should note that the Forest of Arden
appears in one of them. Bit of a clue there, methinks. I like
it when authors use familiar places in their stories,
because the readers get excited by mentions of places they
know, don't you agree? Anyway, then we drove through
Wootton Wawen (very strange name), past Snitterfield to
our left, where Shakespeare's dad was from, and where
Bill the Quill went a-boozing with his playwright mate,
Ben Jonson, and further down the road on the right, Mary
Arden's farmhouse (Shakespeare's mom to you), before
we hit the main drag into town. I was not quite as familiar
with the place as David was, so he'd promised to give me
a guided tour before we got down to business. All work
and no play makes Jack a dull boy, and all that. We parked
up on the huge car park next to the leisure centre and
strolled the short distance into town, over the bridge and
the River Avon, which was full to bursting point with
handsome swans, Canada geese and mallard ducks. We
had a quick peek at the Birthplace in Henley Street, and
David told me a killer story about when he painted his
400th anniversary portrait of the Bard for Stratford Town
Council. Yes, of all the artists in the land, they chose him.
He was very proud. Apparently, he'd asked his mate,

Simon, to don the Tudor outfit he'd hired, and pose in the bedroom of the Birthplace for the body reference photographs. This was the room William was actually born in, so it was of symbolic significance as a backdrop for the portrait. Simon sat at a desk with his quill pen, doing what David asked of him, as Steve the photographer snapped away. The only problem was, they'd arrived very late, due to road-works on the M42, and the Birthplace was due to open in ten minutes. Session completed, Simon removed his pantaloons, and was standing in the middle of the room with his, erm, codpiece on show, when a coach-load of Chinese tourists burst in and started taking photos of him and his manhood, much to his embarrassment.

We didn't go inside the Birthplace this time, as we had lots more to do, but the anecdote more than compensated for that. Next, we strolled down the High Street to the Town Hall. David took me inside this lovely old Tudor building, and by pure chance, we met the lady mayor, who knew David, and gave him a nice hug. Then we bumped into the town clerk, and she gave him a hug too. I was beginning to feel a tad jealous. He took me to the bottom of the staircase, once all the random town hall women had had their fill of him, and there, right up high on the wall, was his portrait, and I swear, I saw a tear well up in his eye. He said that, in years to come, when he had shuffled off his mortal coil and gone to that undiscovered country from whose bourn no traveller returns, that portrait would still be in Stratford, where it would become part of the great Shakespeare Story, and he was chuffed senseless to have been a tiny part of it. Next we went to a room where

47

the past mayors' names were all sign-written onto oak panels, a bit like you see in posh golf clubs, with their past presidents. He pointed out a name halfway down one panel. John Shakespeare, Will's dad, a glove-maker who ended up in debt. It was probably when M&S opened down by the river and sold them cheaper than he could. Business can be cruel, don't you think?

All this culture was making me hungry, so we adjourned to Hathaway's Tea Rooms, just down the High Street from the Town Hall, where we had toasted cheese and ham sandwiches and a pot of tea, before strolling down Sheep Street to the Royal Shakespeare Theatre, which stood majestically right next to the Avon. This was where it got *really* interesting. I was a bag of nerves. We walked into the foyer and David asked a lady there if Mike Flowers was around. She said he'd be back in a few minutes, as he'd popped out to get a sandwich. Just as she said it, in he walked, accompanied by his sandwich, and he spotted David immediately and marched over, grinning from ear to ear.

'Bloody hell!' he laughed, 'have you come to get some culture at last? What on earth are you doing here?'

David shook his hand and introduced me. We shook hands too, and then David got down to business.

'Adam, this is my old mate, Mike. He works here, though quite what the old bugger does is beyond me. We met when I was painting the portrait back in 2015 and we got on. Anyway, I'll get to the point, Michael. Did you see that article about an eccentric old artist called Michael Waldron, who committed suicide in jail?'

Mike frowned. 'Didn't he want paying for a picture he did for a duke or something, and the duke said he'd never heard of the chap?'

'That's the one. He was an earl actually, but that's near enough. Well, Adam and I were fascinated by this odd tale, and to cut a long story short – and some might say it's already too late for that – we struck lucky. The chap got sent to jail because he borrowed a Canaletto from the earl as a protest for not being paid, and the Heritage Trust would like it back. We discovered a cryptic clue, written by the artist, which led to another, and another, and another, and another - okay, that's enough anothers, and the last clue led us to this theatre.'

'You're joking!'

'No, I'm not. He came here to watch Hamlet, and sat in row B, seat 2, and we think the next clue might just be hidden in that seat. Could we take a look?'

Mike had rather a lot to take in, but he got the gist.

'God! It's like an episode of "Murder, She Wrote," he laughed.

He scratched his head in disbelief and asked us to follow him into the theatre, so we did, and in a few seconds, we were walking down the aisle towards the stage, and I, for one, wasn't breathing properly. I felt a bit wobbly, like

49

my 'too too solid flesh' was melting. Incidentally, I believe Shakespeare wrote 'sullied' but we'll leave that for now. We reached the seat in question, and I took a huge breath to steady myself.

'The cleaners go round all these once the audience has gone,' said Mike, 'so don't build your hopes up too much.' I got down on my hands and knees and felt around. There was nothing on the bottom – you'd have seen that when the chair was folded up. I shoved my hand into the fold between the seat and the back panel and slid it along slowly, from left to right. Nothing, and then, just as I was arriving at the other side, an obstruction. I looked up at David and Mike, and I swear I saw and heard David gulp. I shoved my hand deeper into the crevice, so to speak, and then forced whatever it was upwards. A piece of white paper became visible. I removed my hand and grabbed it, yanking it out.

'Oh my God!' said Mike. 'What does it say?'

It said:
> **You are doing well, but**
> **don't get tunnel vision.**
> **What better than a canal next,**
> **as you're looking for a Canaletto.**
> **There are more around these parts**
> **than in Venice, they say.**
> **I trust you know which one.**
> **Get a pot of tea, look for The Artist,**
> **your prize is there.**

The three of us stared incredulously at each other. We were in shock. Mike suggested we had a caffè latte at his expense, to calm us down a bit, while he ate his sandwich. We did, and it did.

'Does it mean the canal here, in Stratford?' asked Mike.

'Maybe,' replied David. 'There's one just over there.'

'For once, Sherlock,' I said. 'I know the answer to this one, I think. I may be wrong, but I reckon he's taking us back close to where we live now. He always uses his words cleverly, does he not? That word 'TRUST' for example. The Canal and River Trust have a café, known as Bumble Hole Visitors' Centre. It's in Netherton, not far from the Netherton Tunnel. David, I believe that this is his final clue. It says 'your prize is there'. Surely, this means the painting. And yesterday, in his flat, I found a single key with a key fob that had, "The Artist" written on it, remember? I've got it here, look. I don't know what that bit means yet, but I'll bet you any money, we have to look around that café, or in the tunnel maybe.'

David was convinced. It all made sense, and we were gradually beginning to understand Mr Waldron's thought processes. We stood up, said thank you and goodbye to Mike, and promised to keep him up to speed. Then we skipped back to the leisure centre, chatting animatedly as we walked, like a pair of kids on their way home from school. We both sensed that this was nearly over, which was exhilarating. Then, as we approached the red BMW, David interrupted our chat to ask me what was attached to his windscreen. It was, on closer inspection, a £100 fine from Stratford District Council's parking people, for not buying a ticket. In our excited state, we'd totally forgotten to do so. I examined it, and told David it wasn't all bad news. If he paid today, it would be reduced to £75. Strangely, this bit of good news seemed to do very little to lift his spirits.

Chapter 8
The Artist

I was on my own in Netherton. David had promised to go shopping with Suzanne – look, let's call her Sooz from now on, like David does, to avoid confusion with Countess Suzannah. If this story had been a work of fiction, as a professional writer, I'd have changed one of the names to Mary or something, but as this was real, I was forced to use their actual names, even though I can see how confusing it might get for you. So Sooz it is from this point onwards. Anyway, Sooz insisted that he spent some time with her instead of his new platonic boyfriend, so to placate the woman, he had to look around the Boundary Mill retail outlet, or whatever they call it, and let her buy yet another pair of jeans she didn't really need. And I like the woman a lot, let's be clear. It was David who phrased it that way, not me. A pair of jeans now and again is a small price to pay for living with that bloke!

I parked the car and strolled across a field to the path that separates the lake and canal at Bumble Hole, which, let me tell you, is an eccentric place. There's an old pub, and several other buildings, though I couldn't tell you what they were used for. Outside were loads of old enamel advertising signs, rusty bikes, statues, ornaments, and a proper old gypsy caravan – the sort that horses would pull. I half expected Jay Blades and his team to be inside, restoring them all. I smiled to myself and continued along the path to the bridges that span the canal. They were lovely old cast iron ones, and the entire vista was straight out of the industrial revolution. Canals, a couple of small lakes, a huge chimney stack and the famous Netherton tunnel, which, from memory, is around a mile and a half long, cutting right through a big hill. I've walked through it in the past and it's a bit creepy. Just a canal on your left, with a hand-rail, the sound of dripping water coming from the ceiling, and darkness. Luckily, you can see the exit at the other end, which gives you something to aim for. I'd hate to bump into a psychopathic killer coming the other way, which reminds me; I must do something about my over-active imagination. The tunnel takes you from Netherton to Dudley Port, Tipton, by the way. What puzzles me, though, is why anyone would tunnel *into* Tipton. Before I get a load of angry emails from Tiptonites, I must explain that I do this mainly to annoy David, because he went to Tipton Grammar School, which sounds to me like an oxymoron, similar to 'Police Intelligence' or 'Pretty Ugly'. Just think. Latin and Greek lessons, a headmaster with a gown and a mortar board. In Tipton. And it's just occurred to me. Maybe they were tunnelling *out* of Tipton and trying to escape to Netherton. Jeez! They must have been desperate.

I crossed the ornate old bridge and began to walk towards the tunnel. On my right was the building I was looking for, the Bumble Hole Visitors' Centre, which sold coffee and tea, and various snacks. Inside it was more like a tiny museum, full of interesting bits and pieces of canal memorabilia. I ordered a coffee and asked the lady if she knew what or who 'The Artist' was. She told me that there was a very run-down and scruffy narrowboat opposite us, alongside some very nice ones, that was called 'The Artist', and it was owned by a very run-down and scruffy artist chap who she thought was called Mick. She added that the last time she had seen him in the café was quite a time ago. He was with a very posh-sounding man who was carrying a large postal tube. I thanked her profusely, exited the café and headed back to the ornate bridge. I crossed back to the other side, and strode purposefully to 'The Artist'. Run-down was being polite, having seen it. It was in a sorry state. I must say, though, that the signwriting was very professional, or at least, once-upon-a-time it was. I expected no less if Michael Waldron had done it. I glanced around me to make sure no one was watching, and then slipped over the back of the boat into the lowered little deck where the door was, next to the traditional stripy tiller. I took the key from my pocket and tried it in the door lock. It fitted. I twisted it clockwise, and pushed at the door. At first it wouldn't budge, but it was just stiff. My second attempt opened it, and I ducked down and entered. The smell was interesting; a cross between urine, cider, old sweat, and damp. I examined all the storage spaces thoroughly, but there was no sign of a Canaletto painting, which was very disappointing indeed. I plonked myself down at the table to sit and think awhile, and for reasons best known to myself, took the lid off the old green teapot that was minding its own business in the middle of the Formica table. Inside was a plastic food bag, and inside that, another small envelope. I was sure that this time I had reached my final destination, but alas, it was yet another bloody clue. It read:

Who was Canaletto anyway?
Read all about him!

These clues were getting vaguer and vaguer, or more and more vague, if you are a grammar pedant. How on earth was I supposed to fathom that one out? I pocketed the envelope so I could run it past David the following day. Then I just sat there, staring out of the grimy window for ages, deep in thought. The only way to read about Canaletto was from an art book, and the best way to get an art book was from a library. Was it possible that he'd left a note in a book, and if so, was it in a library, and if so, which library? Stourbridge was the obvious choice of course, and Michael Waldron seemed to be keeping it local, for his sake more than ours, probably.

Then my thoughts turned to the old clapped-out narrowboat – and for those of you who like to refer to them as barges, please don't try that on with a boater or he might stove your skull in with a shovel. Had it been mentioned in Waldron's will, or had he and everyone else forgotten about it? Reverie over, I stood up to leave and whacked my head on the low ceiling, bringing back lovely memories of that cricket ball and my stay in A&E. Temporarily dazed, I exited through the stiff old back door, tried to jump onto the towpath, tripped on the metal edge of the boat and ended up covered in mud and flat out on the wet grass, much to the amusement of a passing couple, walking their Jack Russell, who leapt onto my back and stuck his horrible tongue in my ear. David would have absolutely loved it; seeing me suffer, I mean, not having a Jack Russell tongue in his ear.

I drove home and immediately rang him on his mobile to give him the news, good and bad. We had not located the painting after all, but instead, yet another clue. He agreed that our best bet was Stourbridge library, so we arranged to meet at 10 a.m., but when I told him about the old boat, he asked if I'd mind returning there first so he could take a look at it. It turns out that he'd fancied buying an old boat to do up as a retirement project, and if no one else had claimed it, or been left it in the will, he would make an offer for it. He was particularly intrigued when I told him it was called 'The Artist'. David's life had been full of weird coincidences, and here was yet another. To illustrate this, here are a random pair of mad coincidences for you. At grammar school he lost his beloved clarinet. He was, according to him at any rate, a grade-eight classical clarinettist. He would be, wouldn't he? His parents had paid more than they could afford to get him a good instrument for his ninth birthday, and the loss of it at the age of eighteen deeply distressed him. He got over it and began to play guitar instead, as young men tend to do; it was sexier than a clarinet, he reckoned, but aged twenty-six and recently married to Sooz, he decided to buy another one. To this end, he visited a Dudley music shop and asked the owner if he had any good quality, second-hand b-flat clarinets for sale. David was in luck. A Boosey and Hawkes Emperor, ebony and silver model had been sold to them literally ten minutes before he arrived. David took one look at the case and the instrument and informed the astonished shop owner that it was his missing, presumed stolen one. The thief had waited eight years before deciding to sell the thing, only to have the legal owner walk into the shop ten minutes later and reclaim it. Stranger still, they discovered a hidden note under the vacuum-formed inner section of the box, where the dismantled clarinet sat, echoing Michael

Waldron's clue-laying technique, with 'David Day, 3, Anne Road, Brierley Bank, Staffs' written on it. Thanks to the proprietor's excellent description of the man who brought in the stolen instrument, they were able to ascertain that he was, in fact, the school-caretaker's son.

When David was just eleven years old, he had been asked by his headmaster to create a plywood sheep for the nativity play. He spent weeks and weeks jig-sawing a sheet of plywood into the shape of a sheep, until it was sheep-shape and Bristol fashion. He then mounted it on a stand, and painted it with his dad's Dulux enamels. On the night of the play, the purple velvet curtains of Brierley Bank Junior School's stage opened to reveal David's sheep and three shepherds with tea towels on their heads, sat washing their socks by night, all seated on the ground, when the angel of the Lord came down from the ceiling, spinning wildly on a rope, and booted the sheep into the orchestra pit, where it landed on David's head as he played the recorder, giving him a nasty gash. Andy Warhol referred to 'fifteen minutes of fame', but sadly, David's sheep had only enjoyed fifteen seconds of it before disappearing from view, and beaning his creator in the process.

Then, some forty years later, after giving a talk at his old school, and jokingly asking the new head-mistress for his sheep back, after regaling those present with his silly nativity tale, and consequently being told there wasn't a cat's chance of that happening, the caretaker walks past them carrying a plywood sheep under his arm, and informs the stunned gathering that he's just been cleaning out the area under the stage and found a sheep at the back, covered in cobwebs, so he's going to chuck it in the skip.

There were many more David Day coincidences where those came from, but you get the idea. The man was not only a chaos magnet, but also a coincidence magnet.

Chapter 9
The Library

David picked me up from Wollaston village, as we locals still like to call it, and we set off for Netherton. Sooz, he explained, had gone to Keep Fit with her mate. The thing I most enjoyed about our car journeys was the conversations, which would flit from meaningful to downright bizarre, to highly comic, without warning. Our first topic that day was the long 'A' sound, which we both have a pathological hatred of.

'Why' asked David, 'don't posh folks say *cart* instead of cat? How do they know when to employ the long 'A' and when not to? Why don't they say *marn* instead of man? Or *bart* instead of bat, as in cricket *bart*.'

'Dunno!' I added, unhelpfully.

'And I couldn't go out with a tattooed girl, or one who smoked,' he said, apropos of nothing. 'What about you?'

'Nor me,' I said, 'or someone who pronounced aitch as *haitch*.'

'Oh Christ, no, me neither,' he replied. 'Or said "I literally fell apart when my hamster died," or whatever, when they obviously didn't. Non-literal literallys are a real no-no!'

'And how do you feel about ginger hair?' I asked.

'I don't get worked up about that. I like the Irish Coleen look as it happens.'

'What about Prince Harry though?' I asked.

'Ah, that's different. Anyway, it's him, not his hair that annoys me, and don't start me on that Markle woman.'

'What about women who pump their lips up like a dinghy and paint on those Groucho Marx black eyebrows?' I enquired.

'I'd take people who say "haitch" over that anytime. At least you could stand half a chance of converting them to saying "aitch", by convincing them that they sounded like a dumb, ill-educated turd. They might see reason if they learnt that it was *hugely* frowned upon. They probably just don't realise, because they're ignorant.'

We also touched on Mrs Malaprop people who say 'on tenderhooks' instead of tenterhooks, 'Adeedas' instead of Adidas, 'marshmellows' instead of marshmallows, and pronounce lingerie as 'larnjeray' instead of 'lanjeree'. In the latter case, that means most of the bloody country.

'Stop! Stop!' he cried, 'this is torture! I'm grammar-sensitive. Change the subject.'

He then told me about his new hobby, soap-making. He collected all the old slivers (not slithers) of Pear's soap, chopped them up, melted them in the microwave and then poured the golden liquid into a small jelly-mould-type of

61

thing he found in the shed, in order to make a new bar, which he reckoned looked a bit like a scaled-down version of Ayers Rock in Australia, but it worked okay. This from a chap who used to earn £70,000 a year even back in the 1990s. Oh yes, and he suspected that the management were using uneaten sheets of smoked salmon to line their urinals with, after spotting a row of suspect circular orange items in the four individual stand-up urinals at Marks & Spencer in Kidderminster. With David, you never quite know if he's joking or serious. After that, we nearly crashed his car laughing at one of Sooz's many accidental sexual euphemisms. She'd recently got herself a new-fangled air-fryer, and with a straight face, informed her husband that she was going to shove some pork in her Ninja when they got home.

Then, after a few more similar cringeworthy examples best not repeated here, the conversation became rather more serious, as our thoughts turned to Michael Waldron again. I was beginning to think that he was a hell of a character. Determined, principled, talented, but sadly no longer with us, thanks to that shitbag earl. Half of me wanted to throttle Michael for putting us through this, and the other half wanted to succeed for him.

David agreed, but reminded me of what a complex, moral quagmire this sorry saga was. Even Jesus would have struggled. In his opinion, the only way to end all this successfully was to find *two* paintings, not just one, and thereby prove Michael's innocence.

'Bloody hell!' I replied, 'One is hard enough. I wouldn't mind if the earl was starving, but I visited that Eggington Hall place, and I'm no expert, but I reckon he had £160,000,000 worth of oil paintings on two walls alone, never mind the rest of the building, and they own a house on an island in Italy. So £15,000 wouldn't kill him, *if* indeed he owes it. And we still don't know if that's true, do we?

'They have another place in Italy?' asked David. 'That's my favourite place. I used to work there for a company, on and off for over ten years. We were based in a beautiful place called Stresa, on Lago Maggiore.'

'What?' I asked, my mouth gawping like a fish out of water. 'But that's where *their* place is. I'm sure of it. Stresa she said. They live on an island called —'

'Isola Bella. You are kidding me? I know it back to front. And the other two islands. I used to stay at The Regina Palace Hotel in Stresa, right next to the lake, or else in Arona, a few miles further around it. Bloody hell! Another strange David Day coincidence. As you know, I was a high-end art restorer as well as an artist in my own right, and I was employed by a firm called Caleffi to restore ancient church frescos and Renaissance paintings. They were based in Borgomanero, near Stresa. I was a regular visitor for over ten years, and nowadays, Sooz and I occasionally go on holiday there. It's idyllic!'

I doubt if there has ever been such a profound and significant conversation on a car journey between

Wollaston and Netherton in their long histories, let alone one that managed to cover as many diverse topics. We pulled up in a side-street, locked the car – well, it was Netherton after all – and walked to the fields I had walked through only the previous day. I showed him the madness that was Bumble Hole, and then we headed for the old narrowboat. David stood and stared at it for a long time, holding his chin. He was prone to doing this. Then he looked inside and did the same again. I showed him where the clue was hidden and he smiled. What was it about artists and tea, he wondered. Then we left, locked up and began to walk back to the car.

'I might put an offer in for that old boat,' he said. 'I believe in fate, after all the coincidences that happen to me, They should call me the Coincidence Kid. How can I refuse a boat that's already called "The Artist", when that's what I wanted to call *my* boat, if I ever got one? I'll ask the solicitor if I can offer ten grand, as it needs a lot of loving care and expense to restore it. I need something to do nowadays, especially when this latest investigation is over, if it ever is. Otherwise, Sooz will make me watch "Doctor Jeff, the Rocky Mountain Vet", or "Pitbulls and Parolees", or "Tipping Point" all afternoon, and I'll go quietly mad, like she has.'

We drove back to Stourbridge and parked up in the underground car park which served the giant Tesco supermarket and the Crown Centre, where the library was situated. We jumped onto the escalator, got a ride up to the top floor, and strode purposefully into the library; we were men on a mission. I stepped up to the reception desk and was met by a nice lady called Jan. I knew this was her name because her little badge told me so. I was thrilled to see they hadn't also added her personal pronoun. I like to work them out all by myself.

'Can I help you?' she enquired with a smile. I asked her where the art section was, as I needed to get hold of a book on Canaletto. Luckily, I was still a library member and had remembered to bring my card with me, unlike David.

She said, 'Art lovers, you two?'

It suddenly dawned on me that she thought we were gay. Well, you would, I suppose. I went a bit red and replied, 'No, we're not gay, Jan!'

'She never said we were, you giant turd!' said David, looking as nonplussed as Jan did. I just went a shade redder, from Vermilion to Alizarin Crimson on the blushometer, and shut up.

'We're doing a bit of research on Canaletto for a project we're involved in,' said David, ploughing on regardless. 'I shouldn't be telling you this, but we're trying to track down a stolen painting of his, and we wondered if it might be shown in one of the books.'

'Sounds intriguing,' said Jan. 'Actually, an interesting character took a book out last year on Canaletto. I only remember because he looked like an ageing hippy, and I asked him, "Canaletto fan, are we?" which, on reflection, was a stupid question, and he said, "Yeah! I'm going to steal one soon, so I want to see which one to nick." I just laughed, thinking it was the usual daft banter I have to deal with on a daily basis.'

David and I looked at each other, and we both said 'Hmmmm!' in unison.

'Anyway, follow me!' said Jan, and we did. She knew exactly where the Canaletto books were, and there were four of them currently available. Then she smiled a nice smile, at me in particular, I thought, turned on her heels, which made her long curly hair swish about in a rather pleasing way, and headed back to the reception desk to continue doing whatever librarians did all day.

David took all four books out and we sat at a nearby table to browse through them. Three were softback books, and one was an expensive-looking weighty hardback with library film over the cover to protect it. To my mind, this one was the one to investigate first, as the library film and the book's dust cover were ideal places to hide a note. We'd found so many of these things now, we knew the routine. David carefully peeled away the sticky tape that held the film in place, while I flicked through the other three books and found bugger all. Looking around us in furtive fashion, to make sure Jan didn't return and give us a bollocking for trashing her book, we slipped off the film and dust cover, and to our absolute joy, a piece of paper fell out. No envelope this time, just the paper, probably so that its shape couldn't be seen through the outer protective layers, and thereby encourage unwanted attention from nosy librarians.

'What's it say? What's it say?' I hissed.

'It says,' he replied, taking a deep breath:

I wanted to send you to Stonehenge, but I decided to keep it local.

'What the bloody hell does *that* mean?' I asked, totally deflated as usual, my post-cryptic-clue-reading default position, 'How many more of these blasted things do we have to solve? I'm getting sick of it.'

David held his chin in his hand again, his own default position for deep thinking.

'This, Watson, is a four-pipe problem,' he eventually said.

I told him that I didn't understand a word he was saying. He explained that Sherlock Holmes rated his problems by how many pipes he had to smoke before the answer dawned on him. News to me. Never read any of it.

'Of course, it's obvious!' he said after what seemed like an hour. 'We have our own Poundland version of Stonehenge in Clent.'

'Bloody hell, we do indeed!' I said, uplifted now. 'The Four Stones.'

Stourbridge is a town sitting between two lovely beauty-spots, Clent Hills, and Kinver Edge. On the top of Clent Hills is one of those ancient megalithic sites with four tall, thin, upright stones, where once-upon-a-time, tattooed tribesmen in loincloths probably sacrificed a goat, a naked virgin, or whatever they had to hand at the time. Only this place, it turns out, was a fake. It was, in fact, created in 1763 by the eccentric George Lyttleton, owner of Hagley Hall, which is very similar to Eggington Hall in Staffordshire, as it happens; your typical Palladian mansion in millions of acres. He also had a ruined castle made to amuse himself. Well, there was no telly in those days. A folly, as they were called.

We put the other books back, and left in a bit of a hurry with the posh, heavy hardback one, after thanking Jan and telling her she had been more than helpful. We needed to take that one with us, as David had leafed through it and found the very picture that had been stolen. 'View of the Grand Canal, Venice, looking north-east to the Rialto Bridge, 1724'. Catchy title. As I mentioned earlier, virtually all of Canaletto's other paintings had the same title too, or similar. The description said it was purchased by William Billingham, 4th Earl of Eggington. What made the entry even more interesting was a blue biro circle drawn around the text, presumably by our friend Michael Waldron. Incidentally, Giovanni Antonio Canal was Canaletto's real name. Which begs the question, did he paint canals because it was his surname? And had he been

68

called Giovanni Antonio Rivero, would he have just painted rivers? I just know you want to ask why he was known as Canaletto, so I'll tell you. Canaletto means 'little canal'. His dad was 'big canal', so he was nick-named 'little canal'.

I did make a mental note to pluck up the courage to ring Jan the librarian, and ask her if she fancied having dinner with a novelist; books being her chief interest. I could take her off the shelf, study her at leisure, and return her within three weeks to avoid a fine, once I'd gone through her thoroughly. This wasn't the right time, though, as David was fired up and wanted to go to Clent before darkness descended upon us. I was currently without a woman in my life after Helen, my nurse girlfriend that lived a few doors away, decided to emigrate to Canada to further her career. We were both upset, but obviously her career was more important than I was, so off she went. Anyway, there's no time to explain my convoluted love life, because I have a cracking story to tell, with a killer ending, so the best thing you can do is get hold of my novels, 'The Curious Tale of the Missing Hoof', 'Mr Māori Goes Home', 'Losing the Plot' and 'A Remarkable Chain of Events', my other adventure with David, and all will be explained. I guarantee you will laugh till it hurts too, or your money back.

So we left Stourbridge and drove the relatively short distance to Clent. David parked up at the bottom of the hill, by the Four Stones Restaurant, which looked very nice, by the way, and we set off up the steep hill at a pace that saw us utterly breathless when we got to the stones.

David is sixty-eight or thereabouts, and I am fiftyish, so we probably overdid it in our excitement. Once we'd recovered, we took in the magnificent views of Worcestershire, Hagley, the Malvern Hills, Clent itself, Bromsgrove; you name it. You can probably see Wales too. It is panoramic and gorgeous. Then we examined the stones. We struggled to see where Waldron could have hidden anything. They were just four stones growing out of the grass, no hidden crevices, no horizontal ones like the Stonehenge ones have; nothing. It did occur to me that he may have hidden the thing down the hill in the bloody restaurant – he was devious like that, so I, being the younger man, volunteered to have a look, just as David said, 'hello, hello, hello, what have we *here* then?'

I walked over to him. He was on his knees, looking at the base of one of the stones, where the grass had grown a little longer. He was pointing to a couple of pretty yellow flowers, growing amongst the grass.

'Touch them!' he smiled. It was a funny time to become florally tactile to that extent, but I humoured him. And guess what – they were artificial. We yanked them out of the ground, and lo and behold, the plastic-coated wire stem was longer than we had expected, and halfway down it was a tightly-rolled note in a plastic bag, that was Sellotaped to it. I cannot tell you the joy this brought to our lives. Up there, on a sunny day, surrounded by wonderful views, with what surely must have been the final clue, or if not, one of the final few. Any more would have been taking the piss.

I nervously unrolled it, impatiently biting at the filthy Sellotape and spitting out dirt. I was past caring about hygiene. Eventually, it was unfurled. It said:

Lovely view, isn't it?
Worth the climb,
and it doesn't take hours!
Now visit my wife,
and take her some flowers.
You are very close now,
whoever you may be!

Chapter 10
The Crematorium

We visited the florist's shop in Stourbridge, and purchased some lovely white lilies. I say we – it was David who insisted on paying for them, bless him. Then we drove to Stourbridge Crematorium. I had done some digging, if you'll excuse the rather poor-taste unintended pun, and found out that Pamela, Michael's wife, had ended her days at the Cobden Hospice, and been buried at the Crem, as we locals call it. I also found out that Michael had reserved a plot next to her for when his time came, and sadly, it came quicker than it should have done. Because he had committed suicide, he would have to be subjected to a *Post Mortem*, though why that was needed, I couldn't say. Surely, the pathologist would conclude that the man had died because of wrist lacerations and a severe lack of internal blood, being as most of his eight pints were on a cell floor in a Staffordshire prison, or else on the wall.

We stood at the grave and bowed our heads, which is an odd response when you think about it, but we all do it, don't we? I then knelt down on a bit of plastic I'd brought with me for that purpose – we were becoming forensically thorough now, like two characters from Silent Witness, and David emptied the vase full of withered, sorry-looking flowers that was there, into the bin provided by the Crematorium. Before placing our nice fresh lilies into the vase, and giving them a drink of water (we remembered to bring that too) he peered inside it but found nothing of interest. However, further examination revealed a tiny, folded piece of paper, wrapped in cling film, taped to the bottom of the vase. It was no more than an inch square, and sat neatly into the base, which was slightly inset, with a rim running around it, so that it housed the note perfectly. For the umpteenth time that fortnight, we looked knowingly at each other for quite a time, but not in a gay fashion, not that there's anything wrong with that, I hasten to add. I opened the package with trembling fingers. The weather had got to it a bit, but it was still readable. It said:

Thank you for her flowers.
Sorry for taking you
on a wild goose chase.

'I don't believe this,' said David, clearly frustrated beyond belief. 'Is this it? Was this whole bloody fool's errand just about putting some fresh flowers on the poor woman's grave?'

Now it was my turn to hold my chin and smoke at least four imaginary pipes.

'I don't believe that,' I replied. 'I just don't. Maybe this is yet another clue and we're not seeing it. We can't rule that out. You know when you watch a quiz show like "The Chase" on TV and they give you four answers to choose from, and one just sort of rings a bell. You often think you don't know the answer, full-stop, but one of those choices keeps nagging at you, like it's somewhere in a dusty old filing cabinet at the back of your mind. Well, that's how I'm feeling about this one.'

73

'And when might you delve into this filing cabinet, pray?' asked David, 'only my knees are killing me.'

'Christ! I don't know,' I said, 'so shall we — hang on. Hang on! You know I went to the hall to look inside the suit of armour. Well, I was over by the space where the Canaletto used to be, just mooching about, and I remember a painting that would have been next to it, to the right. It was different to the other stuff because it was Impressionist in style. Hang on, it's coming to me! Alfred somebody or other. I presumed it was by Monet but it wasn't.'

'Ah, that'll probably be Alfred Sisley,' smiled David. 'He was English but spent his time in France, in the same places that Monet did. His style is very, very similar to Claude Monet; well spotted! But what are you on about, if anything?'

'Well, I was looking at this scene. Very nice, it was. And I'm sure it was called "Wild Geese on the Seine" painted in 1874, and I'll tell you how I remembered that too. My credit card pin number is 1874, and I thought, bloody hell, a David Day-like coincidence.'

'Brilliant!' grinned David, slapping me on the back. 'What superb recall. So *if* you're right, and your dusty filing cabinet isn't talking bollocks, Michael Waldron has sent us all around the Wrekin – well, actually everywhere *but* the Wrekin as it happens – and deliberately made us go full circle, because it appeals to his sense of humour, and now we are right back, literally, and I use the term

74

"literally" literally, next door to where you began, a couple of weeks ago. So I reckon there'll be another clue behind the Sisley, and it will either tell us where the Canaletto is or it'll tell us to eff off.'

'It all fits, doesn't it?' I said, grinning, and thrilled that we'd made what I hoped was a major breakthrough; maybe even the closing chapter in this oddest of tales.

'Look,' said David, 'tomorrow, I'll drive to Eggington Hall, if you can explain to me where it is, and have a nose. If you came inside with me, that Heritage Trust woman would recognise you and call security, so if you want to come for the in-car banter, stay in the car park till I've done my bit. I'll hang around by the Sisley, looking interested, and casually have a feel behind it when she's not looking. While I'm there, I'll also probe her about when the earl and his wife are at the hall and when they're in Italy. I have a cunning plan, as Baldrick used to say.'

'Oh, do tell!'

'Not yet. Let's see what Sisley reveals first, and meanwhile, I want to ring a very old friend to ask for a favour. And another old friend for another one.'

Chapter 11
Back to Eggington Hall

David's swanky BMW rolled into the car park at 10.30 a.m. He got out, took a deep breath, and said, 'Wish me luck!' before striding over to the front entrance and up the steps. Once inside, he made his way to the yellow room, said hello to the lady sat on the uncomfortable chair near the door, and began to meander nonchalantly around the huge room, pausing at oil paintings. He was, thankfully, the only visitor at that time.

'I hear this place is used as a film set,' he called to the Heritage Trust lady.

'Yes,' she replied, 'A lot of these stately homes are jumping on that bandwagon at the moment, thanks to our obsession with period dramas, and it helps pay for the upkeep of these places.'

'Ah yes, I know. I've done a few art restoration jobs for a place called Wrothdale Park in Shropshire, where they filmed some of Downton Abbey, and loads of other period dramas. They do really well out of it too. I bet *they* could afford to pay artists that *they'd* commissioned to do portraits!'

'Sorry,' said the lady, 'I didn't quite get what you meant there.'

'Oh, just a daft private joke,' David smiled. 'Just ignore me.'

'Yes, I am familiar with Wrothdale Park,' she continued. 'They do a hell of a lot of filming there, as you say, whereas we only get bits and pieces from a lot of the same dramas as it happens, but it all helps. Where you're standing now is where Queen Victoria stood talking to the Prime Minister in "Young Victoria". If you look out of the back windows of the green room across the corridor, that stands in for Gatcombe Park, where Princess Anne lives, in "The Crown". And this place was also Aunt Agatha's house in "Jeeves and Wooster". You know, Stephen Fry and Hugh Laurie.'

David was impressed and a little star-struck. He was a huge fan of P.G. Wodehouse, as was I. Interestingly, Wodehouse used to live in a small village called Badger, of all things, not far from the hall. He had also lived not far from Worcester, which is, of course, where he got the name of his most famous character from. The Worcester Evening News used to have a little subtitle on the front cover that read, 'Worcester, pronounced Wooster', probably for the benefit of any visiting Americans who wrongly called it War-Sester. Wodehouse would often switch this around, and say 'Bertie Wooster, pronounced like Worcester'. Reginald Jeeves, his brainy valet, was named after a Warwickshire cricketer. Wodehouse liked going to Edgbaston to watch the county matches and tests, as he was also a keen and half-decent amateur player.

David meandered around the room, gradually getting nearer to where the Canaletto once hung. He could see the Sisley now. It was a lovely Impressionist painting, and he stood in front of it, taking it in.

'Are you an art fan?' the lady asked. That was twice that week he'd been asked that.

'Yes,' said David, 'a professional artist and picture restorer for forty-five years. I retired recently. I worked on what you'd call the big stuff. The world-famous painters. Caravaggios, Constables, Turners, you name it – I even repaired a Leonardo da Vinci once. That was a great cure for constipation, I can tell you! Monets, Van Goghs, Sisleys like this one; I cleaned a Vermeer for the Rijksmuseum in Amsterdam, and hundreds more I won't bore you with.'

It was probably already too late for that, I would have said.

'Goodness me!' she replied, 'I've never met someone who did that before; restoring paintings.'

'Yes, it's a nerve-wracking job sometimes. I've actually restored a Canaletto, for a museum in Venice, ages ago. I'd like to restore *your* Canaletto, but that might not be as easy!'

The lady laughed at his little witticism. 'Yes, the police are getting nowhere fast with that. When I came into the room that day, I thought maybe they'd just taken it off to clean it or whatever, but then I remembered that they did that only a couple of years ago, so they surely wouldn't be doing it again so soon. That time it went missing for several months, but this time, Lord knows if we'll ever see it again. Especially now the chap has died. Anyway, if you'll excuse me for one minute, I need to pop to the loo. Can I trust you not to steal any of the other ones?'

'Of course,' he smiled. I'll guard them for you, and maybe touch a few of them up while you're away. I've brought my paintbrushes!'

He had seemingly won the lady's trust, unlike me, and her weak bladder had been an unexpected bonus. As soon as she left, his hands were fondling Alfred Sisley's backside, a sentence I probably won't ever utter again. There was indeed a note – glory be to God – and it was taped to the bottom right corner. To peel it off and pocket it was, for David, the work of an instant, as Wodehouse used to say. He moved away so he could pretend to study a Titian, pleased with himself and grinning like an idiot as he did so. A few minutes later, the lady returned and sat down. He did his level best to calm his face down and act normally, a difficult task for David.

'Did I miss anything?' she laughed.

'Not really, 'David replied. 'All the paint fell off that Van Dyck over there while you were out, but I put it all back again while you were having a pee. No charge!'

Well, he was three-parts delirious after his find. It was the best he could come up with. Before he left the room, he wandered over to her and asked if the earl and his wife still lived at the hall, now that The Heritage Trust had taken over the running of the place. The lady told him what he already knew, about their bolt-hole on the Italian lake, and added that they were staying at the hall at the moment because the house in Italy was being redecorated, and they'd probably return in a couple of weeks, once it was finished.'

'Oh really?' David replied. 'I might ask him if he has any old masters that he needs restoring. Being retired is so boring!'

And with that, he said cheerio, and left the room.

Back in the car, I was jittery. He'd seemed to be a long time in there. He jumped in, slammed the door and shouted 'YES!' at the top of his voice. He produced the paper, and we read it together in silence.

'Did you read what I just read?' I asked him. 'Am I dreaming this?'

'Let me read it again,' said David, who, without exaggeration, looked in a state of extreme shock and bewilderment.

The note was short, to the point, and dramatic, to say the least. It was fair to say, we did *not* see that coming.

Chapter 12
A Trip Abroad

David rang me quite early on Friday, to fill me in on what he'd been up to. Partly as a result of the dramatic and unexpected final clue, he'd gone into overdrive with his plan. Now here's a good tip. Never answer the phone while you're eating cornflakes. By the time you've hung up, they are a mushy, inedible mess. I lost five portions of them on the trot once when David was ringing me about solving clues one day. On my wages I can't afford it. The other problem with cornflakes is that there's always some milk left, so I add a few extra cornflakes to use it up, only to find I then need some more milk to use the cornflakes up, so I add some more, and then realise that – well, you get the idea. You can go on forever if you're not careful. I daresay people with O.C.D. measure out a very precise amount of milk in one of those measuring jugs, and then count out exactly 347 cornflakes so both items are used up at exactly the same time. Or you could just have some toast instead I suppose. Anyway, he asked 'What are you up to next week? Wednesday to Sunday?'

'Nothing exciting,' I replied. 'Why do you ask?'

'After what we read on the Sisley "Wild Geese" note, we need to get a real move on. When did you last have a few days' holiday?'

'Not for ages, as it happens,' I admitted. 'I haven't been anywhere special since I went to New Zealand yonks ago.

I'm not exactly well off at the moment. The writing game is, shall we say, intermittent. It's as dead as a dodo.'

'Do you like Italian food?'

'Does the Pope shit in the woods?'

'That I couldn't be sure of, I'd need to ask Google, but pack your bags, we're having a mini-break in Italy. Me, you and Sooz.'

I looked at the telephone receiver quizzically. Was this another of David's daft jokes, I wondered.

'Italy? And who is paying for *that*?' I asked.

'I am. I'm going to book flights from Brum to Malpensa, leaving at 10.30 a.m. Wednesday morning. It only takes one hour and forty-five minutes to get there, which is nothing, and then there's a coach to Stresa that they lay on. It's only half an hour or so away from the airport. Stresa has a string of large, posh hotels along the edge of Lake Maggiore, and back in the day, when I worked there, I was always put up at The Regina Palace Hotel, which was built back in 1908 in the grand style. It's a glitzy place with a huge, central staircase, plush rooms, chandeliers, outdoor and indoor swimming pools, beautiful manicured gardens; the works. We're staying just four nights, bed and breakfast. I've been in touch with my old employer and mate, Luca Bonini, who lives just outside Stresa. I asked if he could find out where the earl and his wife live, and he came up trumps in no time. They all know about them on the island, apparently. Casa Tavola, Viale del Palazzo Borromeo, Isola Bella. He went past it yesterday and noticed that the decorators were there, which I already knew about. I've asked him to translate something into Italian for me, because after all those years working there, I can still only swear fluently, and order food and drink. And he's just emailed it to me. I'm printing that onto an official letterhead from Eggington Hall, which I designed myself on Photoshop. It should, with a bit of luck, give us access to the place. This is what it says:

'Dear Sirs, would you please allow my picture restorer, Mr David Day, to come into the house, as he has to collect the portrait of my wife, Suzannah, to apply the final coat of varnish. He'll take it away and have it back the following day for you, all being well.

Thank you,

Charles Billingham, the Earl of Eggington.'

'I don't know what to say!' I gasped. 'That's fantastic! I can't believe it. Thank you, David. So you really reckon he's got the picture stashed away there? It's a long shot, and now it's a very expensive long shot.'

'I know it is,' he admitted, 'but we need a bit of a break, Sooz and I, so I thought we'd combine business with pleasure. If it works, great, if not, we'll have a nice time anyway, I'll show you around my old stomping ground, and we'll go home knowing we did our best, whatever the outcome. As you know, the last bit of that final clue from Michael reiterated that he truly had painted Suzannah's portrait and that the earl was a liar, and I, for one, believe him. Artists have been mistreated from time immemorial, and I want justice for that poor man. No one could find anything back at the hall, even after the police were allowed to search it, so it's a good bet that the earl brought it over to Italy, and hid it at his other place. And if that's true, his bloody wife is no better than he is. Finding the Canaletto just benefits them and the Trust, not Michael. I am determined to find that missing portrait as well, and this is my hunch. Let's go for it!'

I had never been to Italy, and I was very excited about the trip. Very early on Wednesday, David and Sooz picked me up, and we drove down the M42 to junction 6, where you get off for Birmingham Airport. We checked in, had a croissant and a cup of tea, and eventually boarded the plane. I hate flying, if I'm honest, but it was a nice sunny day, the company was good, and in no time, we were descending into Malpensa, Milan, the largest airport in that area. When David used to work in Italy as a picture restorer, years before, he had always flown to Linate airport, the third largest in the area, so he knew both fairly well. The Italian lakes are all only an hour or two from the airports, and there are quite a few of them, all beautiful. He worked mainly around Maggiore, the idyllic, smaller Lake Orta, and of course, in Milan itself. Nearby were Como, Garda, Lugarno and a few smaller ones he could never remember the names of. We cleared customs and hopped onto the shuttle bus for Maggiore. Along the way, he pointed out interesting houses and areas he was familiar with. We passed a house that Madonna had been interested in buying, but eventually didn't, and the house owned by ex-Prime Minister, Silvio Berlusconi, that funny little chap who liked hosting sex orgies, like you do. We arrived in Stresa, which David explained was pronounced 'Strayza', and it looked absolutely beautiful. The lake was twinkling in the sunshine, and all around it were the Italian alps, and grassy hills dotted with fancy villas and mansions. Fabulous vintage mahogany speedboats, like the ones you see in James Bond films, bounced across the water at speed, piloted by bronzed Italian chaps in Ray-Bans, showing off to their gorgeous, bikini-clad women. Sailboats flitted from island to island, and on dry land, the restaurants were full of folks enjoying pizzas and pasta, drinking Peroni and Moretti lagers, and promenading around the markets and along the lakefront. It was Heaven, and this, my friends, was where David had worked for years. It was a hard life. You couldn't help but feel sorry for the poor chap. The bus dropped us off at the front of The Regina Palace Hotel, which was picture-postcard perfect. Either side of it were many more similar grand hotels, all just over the road from the car parks, the lake, and the place where you could hop on a ferry to any of the neighbouring towns, the Borromean islands, or even to Locarno in Switzerland, where the lake ended, sixty-six kilometres away. Lord knows what that is in English money. I'm hopeless. It's a very big old lake, anyway!

We checked in, and David and Sooz went to unpack and have a rest, and so did I. We arranged to meet in an hour, down in the lobby, and decide what to do first. I was very conscious of being the gooseberry, but having been married for something like forty-five years or more, they didn't think that way, and they wanted to show me the sights. My single room was smallish, but very nice, and I had a balcony overlooking the lake. I could see the island just off the shore, and I took this to be Isola Bella, where we were going the following day. Apparently, you jumped on one of the small, canvas-topped motor-boats moored just over the road. They were captained by swarthy Italian blokes wearing those blue, peaked caps with gold-braid bands around them and a little anchor at the front, like the ones that dick-heads in England like to wear when they hire a canal boat for a week's holiday. Just to their right were the bigger passenger ferries that had a licensed bar and two levels of seating, one inside, and one on top in the sunshine, for longer journeys.

We went for a pizza on the terrace of a lakeside restaurant, and sat in the warm sun, watching the boats float by. It was truly idyllic. If I could have upped sticks and lived there immediately, I would have done. I even had a couple of Peroni lagers, which I normally never do in the daytime. Then, David got us tickets for one of the larger ferries, and we set off across the lake to Switzerland, to visit Locarno market. If I had to be brutally honest, it was quite a lot better than being in Dudley market.

The entire afternoon was magical, and so relaxing. We both knew that the following day was when we would have to do what we had come all the way to Italy for, but before that, and hopefully after that, we intended to enjoy ourselves. I still couldn't quite believe that David had paid for it all, and I was truly grateful. After a lovely, if brief time in Switzerland, mooching around the market, drinking coffee and laughing a lot, we noticed that everything was at least three times as expensive, so we caught the boat and returned to Stresa before it got dark and we got broke, with David pointing out the various towns he'd been to in the past, restoring an old church fresco here, and a renaissance painting there. I was deeply envious. He also reeled off the many disastrous but funny incidents he'd been involved in, such as the time he set off from The Regina Palace to walk to a nearby restaurant, shortly after a heavy and unexpected downpour. He rounded a corner, just as a tourist coach did the same but in the opposite direction, hitting a puddle in the road that was only a tad smaller than the lake itself. A tidal wave of filthy, freezing cold water engulfed him and his best suit. He reckoned you couldn't have been wetter if you'd just been dropped off a pier into the sea. Another time, he arrived at the Milan exhibition centre, placed his bag of art equipment on a table, only to see a sneak-thief grab it and run out of the centre into the busy streets and disappear. The bag also contained his new rimless spectacles and his wallet, amongst other important stuff. Luca managed to borrow some specs of approximately the same prescription from his middle-aged secretary, Cinzia, who favoured the type worn by Mary Whitehouse, with sharp pink points at each side, which were adorned with little plastic multi-coloured flowers. For the rest of the week, the poor chap was either too blind to be able to restore his painting properly, or else constantly chatted up by gay Italian men. It was a stark choice.

That evening, we ate at the hotel, drank Primitivo followed by grappa – or Ronsonol, as David calls it – and staggered up the grand staircase to sleep it off. The next day, after breakfast, we had work to do.

Chapter 13
Isola Bella

We were up fairly early, by our standards, and had eaten breakfast by 9.30 a.m. In case you are not aware, Italian hotels all tend to do crap breakfasts. A slice of characterless cake, a few strips of Prosciutto di Parma, weird cereal that looks and tastes like polystyrene, and tea that tastes like dirty water. For a nation that has the best food on the planet, they let themselves down badly with hotel breakfasts. We strolled over to the boats and bought three return tickets for Isola Bella.

As we chugged merrily across the lake, I experienced a strange mixture of emotions. It was a beautiful day, Stresa was magnificent, the locals were friendly, Isola Bella was stunning and approaching fast, but my stomach was churning with nerves. David had his large cardboard box with the blue strips of 'U' section polystyrene inside that they use to protect the edges of picture frames, his Nikon camera; the same one Michael had, and a small bag of art materials – brushes, varnishes and so on, just for show. Sooz was wearing her trendy Ray-Bans, and I was wearing the sunglasses my dad gave me, with the lens that keeps dropping out. The captain moored up at the landing stage, and the little boat bobbed about playfully as we tried to get off it. I noticed the captain paid far more attention helping Sooz off the boat than he did with us. Well, he was Italian after all. We walked up the slope onto the footpath, where stalls were selling all manner of tourist stuff, sunglasses, scarves, T-shirts with Stresa printed on the front, pottery and DVDs. There were lovely open-air cafés, those distinctive, tall, pointed Italian Cypress trees, little interesting stone steps in narrow alleyways that led to the higher avenues, and private houses with lovely balconies that were full of those red and pink flowers that the Italians seem to love. Geraniums, are they? I'm hopeless with flowers!

We headed for a pretty café with lovely lake views that David often visited, back in the day, and ordered three cappuccinos, or should I say 'tre cappuccini'. When the waiter returned with them, David summoned up his incomplete knowledge of the Italian language, asked him where La Viale del Palazzo Borromeo was, and the man pointed to it. David said, 'Grazie mille, signor', like a local, and paid for the coffees. He once told me about a friend of his who was about to visit Stresa for a holiday, and was looking for tips on how to pronounce things properly, so he wouldn't look a fool. David might not have the vocabulary; he'll admit that, but he is a human Mynah bird when it comes to pronunciation. He hears things properly and copies them exactly, which gives the listener the impression that he's far better at speaking Italian or German than he actually is. In short, his observational skills are second to none, which is why he is such a brilliant artist. Graham, the man in question, asked about various food words, such as prosciutto (pronounced pro-shooto) and tagliatelle (pronounced tal-yee-atelli) and then they got onto coffee and drinks. David hates when people say 'lartay' instead of 'la-ttay' when ordering coffee, so he drilled this into Graham *ad nauseam*. Then Graham went off to Italy, visited the beautiful Lake Orta, popped into a café and asked for a 'latt-ay', as instructed, and the waitress brought him a pint of milk. In England, we leave out the word caffè. In Italy, they don't.

When we'd finished our drinks, we rose, looked at each other, gulped in unison, and then walked with a determined stride to the beautiful palace, with its spectacular gardens, a few minutes away. We found the small avenue, which ran down the side of the palace grounds, and strolled slowly along it until we saw some activity outside a beautiful, typical Italian townhouse. It had a first-floor balcony with a table and chairs on it, alongside the obligatory terra-cotta pots full of those geranium-type things I mentioned earlier. The ornate, ancient, studded front door was open, and a chap wearing a white decorator's overall was leaving to fetch something or other from his van, which was parked a few yards down the road. David, seizing his opportunity, ran after him and gave him the letter. The man opened it and read it, smiled, they exchanged a few friendly words, and then he handed it back to David. David ran back to us, and he looked pleased.

'All sorted!' he smiled. 'Luca popped in yesterday, as I asked him to, and warned the decorators that a chap would be turning up today to collect an oil painting for varnishing. I've now shown him the earl's letter – I use that term loosely – and all is well. There's only one problem. What if there isn't an oil painting of Suzannah Tavola in there?'

'Christ!' I replied. 'I'd forgotten about that possibility. We'll just look puzzled, and you can try to explain that it must be at Eggington Hall and the earl has made a mistake or something. Good luck with translating that one!'

Sooz had decided that three was a crowd, and elected to mooch around the market and maybe buy a pair of jeans she didn't need. We arranged to meet her in half an hour or so, and, wishing each other luck, we went inside and up the stairs. There were oil paintings everywhere, some by fairly well-known artists, but nothing to compare to what the earl had on his walls back home. We tapped the door of what we presumed was the main living room, and a voice said 'Si accomodi!' which David recognised as 'Come in!' so we did. There were three young men with rollers, paintbrushes and step-ladders, doing decorator-type stuff. The furniture was all covered up with white sheets. They were friendly, and all said hello. The man that David had shown the letter to seemed to be explaining it to the others. We said hello back, and began scanning the room for the oil painting. There was nothing that fitted the description, or indeed the reference shot on Michael's Nikon D40.

David, in his best Italian, asked about other rooms.

'Un dipinto é Suzannah Tavola, per favore? Un'altra stanza, possibilmente?'

'Ah, si!' said the one that David had met in the street. He walked to the doorway and turned right, down the corridor. He opened another door which led to a dining room. We both followed him inside, and he pointed to it, above the fireplace. I felt my legs turn to jelly.

'Perfetto!' smiled David, 'Grazie!' and the man turned on his heels and left us to it. It was her alright, the same pose as the one on Michael's camera. The painting was beautifully framed, as one would expect from Frinton's, David assured me, and beautifully painted, as one would expect from Michael Waldron. There was another subtle clue that it was the one we were looking for. It was signed by Michael Waldron and dated. We looked at each other, and then, quite unexpectedly, we gave each other a huge manly hug that lasted ages. I swear David had a tear in his eye again. He's a serial weeper, the big girl! He went over to the painting, gently lifted it off its wall-hook and then we carefully applied the blue polystyrene frame-protectors and taped them together at the corners. Then David slipped it into his tough cardboard box. He was breathing heavily, in through his nose and out through his mouth. This was the culmination of all our efforts over the last few weeks, and a moment to be celebrated, but perhaps, not where we currently stood. That would hopefully come later. David taped the box shut, and we returned to where the men were busy decorating.

'Grazie!' we both said – I could just about manage that bit – and David added 'Torno presto!' or 'back soon', which was a bloody lie. Like Elvis, we left the building, and headed for the market where hopefully he could intercept Sooz before she bought any more jeans. That didn't go to plan, as she'd already got two pairs in a bag, but our main objective had been achieved, and we were ecstatic. We took the painting back to The Regina Palace and locked it in David's room. Then we went out for lunch. David took us out on another boat, this time to nearby Arona, where he often used to stay in the Atlantic or Concorde hotels. He is always entertaining; I have to admit. He told me about the time he was taken by Luca to a nice restaurant in Arona after work. It was a set menu, and the first course was a tiny plate of spaghetti, which he devoured in seconds. Still hungry, he asked if he could have more, a bit like a Black Country version of Oliver Twist, so the waiter, who looked a tad puzzled, according to David, brought him more, which he also wolfed down. He'd been hard at it all day, it was 8.30p.m. and he was starving. Luca had just disappeared to the lavatory at that point, and had returned to find his English friend finishing off a great big plate of spaghetti that he had asked the waiter for.

'You do realise that this is an eight-course meal, don't you?' he asked David. Then, course by course, the food kept coming, until David's stomach resembled a beach ball and he was looking queasy. Apparently, after a sleepless and uncomfortable night, his morning bowel movement was, in his words, spectacular. A bit like Vesuvio in 79 A.D.

Arona was nice, lots of trendy shops in a long arcade, and a pretty square at the end of it, surrounded by bars and restaurants, with loads of people eating, drinking and chatting in the sunshine, as the lake twinkled in the background. Over the other side of the water, was Rocca d'Angera, an old castle on the hill which I recognised

94

from a lovely oil painting that David had done, that was hanging in his living room. That evening we decided to forsake the hotel dinners, good as they were, and opted for a local place in the fabulous little shopping area to the left of the big hotels, down a labyrinth of little alleyways. At the centre of them was a piazza, full of outdoor restaurants in the middle section that also had an indoor version around the perimeter, just in case it ever rained. I thought I'd died and gone to heaven. On Saturday, we took a bus to Orta, where Luca had a lakeside boathouse. Imagine a big, blue-brick, square building, decorated in the Italian style, with the living space and balcony on the top two floors, and instead of a garage under your house, occupying the ground floor, it's the lake, with your Lamborghini mahogany speedboat bobbing about next to a wooden landing stage.

Orta was delightful, and very old. There was an island in the lake, just like in Maggiore, so we went to have a look. There was an old church there, and inside was a high plinth with a glass top, and in it was a dead pope, or some such top church person - a bishop or cardinal maybe - just lying in state there for all to see, in his pope regalia, his body preserved in special pope-preserving fluid. Jeez, it was weird. I couldn't get that image out of my head all afternoon. We had lunch in one of the lakeside restaurants that seem to be suspended on poles above the water, so boats can moor there. Then we returned to Stresa to eat and drink some more, once we had indulged in an ice-cream each, from one of the many gelaterias, and had a lie down. A chap at the hotel told me that grappa was actually good for the digestion, so I reluctantly drank several that night for that reason only, and woke up with a full beard and covered in badly-spelt tattoos, in Romania.

We were flying home on Sunday evening, but we still had enough time to take in a few more sights, so David suggested we walk the short distance to the cable car. This takes you up to the summit of Mottarone. There are a couple of restaurants and cafés at the top, where you can sit outside and admire the incredible panorama. You can see the seven local lakes, Maggiore, Orta, Mergozzo, Comabbio, Monate, Varese and Biandronno. I think the famous ones such as Garda and Como are a tad further away and not visible. We had a lovely time, and it was a great way to say a tearful farewell for the time being to David's favourite place on earth. It was a wonderful way to remind ourselves that we had to live life to the full, while we could. His beloved dad had died at sixty-seven, as had Sooz's dad, and David had just turned sixty-eight. He wasn't sure if he had years to go or was living on borrowed time.

It was Thursday, the 13th of May, 2021, and this turned out to be extremely poignant for the three of us. If we'd have decided to go to Italy the *following* week, and ride on the cable car at the same time of day, all three of us would have been killed.

Chapter 14
Another Trip to Eggington Hall

On Monday, the 17th of May, we were waking up in the West Midlands again, after an incredible four days in the Italian Lakes. We had achieved our goal, and stolen back Michael Waldron's painting, which made us feel vindicated and rather proud. We could have gone all that way to discover that no such painting existed, and concluded that Waldron was mad and delusional after all, but in truth, I think we were both absolutely sure, even before the trip, that this wasn't the case.

I am also glad that we didn't delay our visit until the following week, and that David was able to book the tickets right away, for two reasons. That last clue – the one we referred to as the Sisley Clue, or the Wild Geese Clue – revealed something that not only astonished the pair of us, but called for a speedy response.

The second reason was even more dramatic, as I hinted, right at the end of the previous chapter. On the 23rd of May at noon, exactly a week after our trip, at the *exact* time we were travelling on the cable car the previous week, the thing suffered a major malfunction. It then collapsed, smashed into the mountain and killed fourteen of the fifteen people on board. The only survivor, a five-year-old boy, lost his two-year-old brother, his parents and two grandparents. When we saw the TV and read our newspapers a week after our trip, the three of us were in deep shock and very distressed indeed. Some time back, Sooz had visited the Twin Towers in New York with a friend, only to hear that they were later destroyed by deranged and fanatical Islamic suicide pilots. She and David had also spent a lovely time in New Zealand, as had I, not that long after they'd been there, and we'd visited beautiful Christchurch, only to hear that an earthquake destroyed most of it a few years afterwards. We were beginning to think we were all jinxed in some strange way. This latest extraordinary tale of mine, which I've entitled 'The Artist's Revenge' has had its highs and lows, that's for sure. It all sounds too bizarre to be true, but trust me, it was.

David's first job, on returning home, was to ring Chris Smith, a friend of his, who was a senior C.I.D. officer. The pair had met a few years previously, when Chris joined one of David's occasional art classes. He was becoming very stressed with his demanding job, and thought it might be therapeutic for him. Chris was the first to admit that he was hardly Michelangelo, but painting did relax him after a traumatic day at work. David had once given him a watercolour portrait project to hand in at the next monthly class. Chris proudly showed him the results of his hard work, and David, in his usual sarcastic way, had told Chris that the picture was a perfect likeness, but not of the person he'd been painting. David was convinced that it was Rod Stewart, and a red-faced Chris informed him that it was supposed to be Princess Diana. In spite of this, they had remained friends, and David had actually helped the senior police officer to catch the psychopathic killer who committed what were later referred to in the daily papers as 'The Tea Bag Murders'. Now David looked likely to feature in the newspapers yet again, and me with him, in what the tabloid press would probably call 'The Earl, his Wife, and the Canaletto', or maybe they'd just come up with a daft headline such as 'Just One Canaletto, give it to me!'

Chris was told all about the tragic Michael Waldron case in great detail, including the part about the cryptic clues, so he was totally up to speed and champing at the bit to make amends, get Michael an apology and a pardon – for all the good that would do him – and see that the Earl of Eggington was made to pay for his immoral and illegal actions. Chris decided to arrange a meeting with the earl which we would also attend, and David advised Chris to do this as soon as possible, because there was a danger that he would return to Italy. He was going to be told that they had found and were returning his missing Canaletto, to get him enthused about the meeting, and he'd be introduced to the two sleuths who'd actually tracked it down for him. We would then show him another missing painting of his, which he probably wouldn't be quite as enthused about. It was an elaborate trap to catch a rat.

The only possible problem with all that was, neither I nor David had actually seen the missing Canaletto with our own eyes. We just knew, thanks to Michael's final clue, where he said he'd hidden it. If this was just another elaborate ploy, we would all look very silly, but at least we had one of the two pictures for certain, so either way, it was going to be a memorable meeting at Eggington Hall.

I was at a loose end for a few days, while the policemen tried to arrange the meeting, so I finally found time to do something I'd wanted to do for a while. Followers of my adventures will probably remember my faithful companion, Len, the dog, who died, as we're all going to do – sorry to be so cheerful – and in doing so, broke my heart. I had not tried to hastily replace him, because nothing would, but now I felt it was time to rescue another little devil who would probably eat me out of house and home, run up huge vet's bills, scratch my new settee, piddle in the kitchen now and again, chase ducks, shit outside the old bag from the Neighbourhood-Watch's bungalow, and expect me to get it up for him while she neighbourhood-watched from the window, seething, her huge arms folded and looking like Les Dawson in drag. Overriding all that, he would make me happy, and hopefully I'd do the same for him. He'd be someone who'd love sitting on my lap every night after dinner to watch the telly (Len, like Sooz, loved Doctor Jeff the Rocky Mountain vet), get over-excited when his daddy returned home, and love having his little furry head rubbed. So I drove down to the local rescue centre, and cast my eye over all the sad inmates; the poor souls who were in prison for crimes they didn't commit, just like Michael had been, and eventually, after much deliberation, I left with a lovably scruffy young border terrier called Monty. Incidentally, while we're on the subject of dogs, I am gifted, or maybe cursed, with an exceptional sense of smell, like a dog has. I can walk down the canal towpath and smell cannabis in the air, hours after the person who was smoking it has disappeared. I may even retrain as a police sniffer dog if the bottom falls out of the journalism market. I could work at the airports, sniffing the baggage for evidence of cocaine. I just draw the line at being shipped back to the station afterwards in a cage at the back of a police van, and being rewarded for my hard work with a tennis ball to play with.

While I was busy sorting out my new furry friend, Chris had been busy too. He'd arranged to meet the earl at Eggington Hall in two days' time, at 10.30 a.m. I was as jittery as hell, but excited too. On the day of the meeting, I must have gone to the loo ten times, I was that nervous. David called for me and we drove to the hall. Chris was standing by his car, waiting for us to arrive. He had a fellow senior copper with him by the name of Andy Moseley. Chris explained that coppers looked better in pairs; just look at any TV cop programme. David opened his boot and took out the painting we borrowed from Stresa. Andy asked him where the earl's Canaletto was, and he explained that all would be revealed once we were inside the hall. David liked a bit of drama.

We were asked to sit in the yellow room, and told that the earl would be down in a moment. We were seated in the corner by where the Sisley and the Steinway piano were, and also the space on the wall where the Canaletto used to be. The heritage Trust lady asked if we'd like tea, and we said 'No thank you', even though I would have loved one. I think we all realised that, if things got awkward, sipping tea in between terse exchanges might look and feel a bit odd. The lady turned to leave, looked at me, and asked, 'Don't I know you?' and I replied, 'Yes,

I was the chap who looked inside the old suit of armour when you specifically told me not to. Thanks to me ignoring you, we think we've found the Canaletto.' I don't think this went down all that well, and I am glad we refused the tea, as I fear she may have spat in it.

The earl arrived, and he was very earl-like. Mustard-coloured tweedy coat, open-necked shirt with yellow Paisley-pattern cravat, swept-back grey hair, confident stride, posh accent, Church brogues like David owned. That's an expensive make, by the way, not shoes you go to church in. I should have explained that many chapters ago, when David fell in the river. Better late than never!

'Ah, gentlemen, welcome!' he said, proffering his hand for shaking purposes. We all reached forward and took our turn. I wondered if he'd feel quite as welcoming in ten minutes' time.

'My name is D.C.I. Chris Smith,' said D.C.I. Chris Smith. This is my colleague, D.C.I. Andrew Moseley, this is artist and art restorer, David Day, and Adam Eve, a journalist. I'll let David explain things!'

'Good morning,' said David. 'Adam and I were fascinated by the newspaper articles about that chap stealing your Canaletto, and that bizarre, awful bit where he wrote an indecipherable sentence on the cell wall, and then died.'

'Absolutely tragic, the man was clearly deranged,' said the earl, shuddering melodramatically.

'Yes, I agree. Tragic. Adam and I have a bit of a history with this kind of thing,' continued David. 'We're getting a reputation as amateur sleuths, but we just can't help getting drawn in. Neither of us had a clue what the words meant, but Adam here pondered it for ages, and realised that he was saying "Iron, my clothes, Sue Tavama" so he cheekily took a look in the visor of that old suit of armour over there, and lo and behold, there was a clue inside the helmet, which he took with him to show me.'

'My goodness!' said the earl, 'how incredible.'

'Yes, and just like in Agatha Christie books, which Waldron must have read too many of, that clue led to another, which in turn led to another; all very cryptic, but we travelled the length and breadth of the Black Country, collecting them all, and we managed to work them all out. If I remember rightly, there were eleven in total, and the final one was behind that Alfred Sisley, just behind Adam there.'

'So the devil started in the yellow room, and ended in the yellow room!' said the earl. 'He led you a merry dance!'

'Yes, he did,' said David, 'and the final note told us where he'd hidden your painting. Adam, step forward.'

I walked to the grand piano and lifted the lid, hoping to God that it didn't contain another clue to be solved. Inside the piano was an ornate picture frame, and in it was a view of the Grand Canal in Venice. David and I blew out a lot of air from our mouths in relief. He put his hands together like a guinea pig does when it's praying, and said 'Phewee!'

Everyone else just looked flabbergasted. It was like the denouement of a 'Midsummer Murders' episode or something. Especially given the setting.

'So you see, Lord Eggington, Charles Billingham, your Earlship, or whatever I'm supposed to call you, Michael Waldron never actually stole your picture, he just moved it three feet away from where it was hanging on the wall. Those outdoor CCTV shots of him with his black A1 portfolio were a red herring. He was playing games. But we haven't just found one painting for you, we've found two! Adam, please.'

I opened the carboard box, slid out the picture within, and quickly slipped off the protective blue polystyrene strips, before holding it up for all to see, a bit like the porters do in auction houses before the bidding starts. I saw the earl's face change.

'Yes, we went all the way to Stresa, and found the painting of your wife that didn't exist; the one you refused to pay for, even though you own a stately home in two-thousand acres, the tied cottages, a beautiful house in Italy, a speedboat, a Cessna plane, tons of priceless antiques, and conservatively, two-hundred million pounds worth of oil paintings, an Aston Martin, a Range

Rover Discovery and a vintage Jaguar. Did I leave anything out?'

The earl was now apoplectic with rage. His face was bright red. 'You broke into my house?'

'No, we just walked in actually, and said "Ciao" to the decorators, and they let me take it. I told them I was a picture restorer, and now I've restored a picture for you, and found you another one you'd completely forgotten you had. Funny that! So you met Michael Waldron at the Bumble Hole Visitor's Centre, and took a postal tube with you that contained a nice photograph of your wife that you wanted made into an oil painting, as a birthday surprise. He duly paints it, which probably took him three months and cost him a lot of money for the Frinton's frame and the linen canvas, and the enlargement of your photo which Dunn's photo lab did – you know, from the picture he took of your photo in the postal tube, so as not to pester you for a larger one. Then you collected it, took it away with all the reference material, preliminary sketches and so on, to make sure there was no trace of it, apart from a forgotten shot in his Nikon camera – careless! – and you decided not to cough up the fee, for reasons best known to yourself, because that portrait is just stunning, like all his work was. Meanwhile, poor Michael loses his wife, loses his mind, and finally his life, and *you* know they'll all believe the posh earl and not the eccentric artist nutter. Artists throughout history have all suffered because of immoral people like you. And thanks to you, he gets sent to prison for stealing a Canaletto as a protest for not being paid, and gets so despondent that he slashes his wrists and dies, yes, all because of you, when you could probably scrape together fifteen grand by emptying your turn-ups. But before he gets carted away to prison, he leaves a few clues, which attract a pair of clever blokes who like a challenge, and now you'll be going to court. Sorry gentlemen, your turn.'

Chris turned to the earl and spoke. 'I think you know what's coming next, sir. Lord Charles Billingham, I am arresting you for perverting the course of justice. Anything you do say —'

And that was pretty much the gist of it. Chris and Andy took him away in the police car, and we hung the Canaletto back on the wall, and while David stood and admired it, I packed away the countess's portrait for safe keeping.

Then he dropped the bombshell.

'Adam,' he said. 'Come here. This Canaletto is a fake.'

Chapter 15
The Plough

We were sat in the back room of The Plough, David's favourite pub, in Wollaston. We would normally sit in the front room, but the back was empty and we needed a private conversation. I was with David, Chris Smith and Andy Moseley, the police officers.

'I didn't see *that* coming,' said Chris, opening his packet of salted nuts. 'The plot thickens. It's like someone emptied half a kilo of cornflour into it and stirred vigorously.'

'None of us did see it coming,' sighed David. 'Adam and I spend two weeks wading through complex cryptic clues, until finally we're sent right back to the hall, where we find the painting in a piano, right next to where it hung on the wall, and we think, brilliant ploy, well done Michael, game's over, and now we discover it's a fake. Bloody marvellous!'

'So Michael faked it?' asked Andy.

'No, he didn't,' said David. 'Impossible. He took it off the wall and immediately hid it in the piano, where it lay for a few weeks till Adam and I cracked the various codes. To fake a Canaletto would take me around three months of hard graft, if not more. Canaletto was a brilliant painter of buildings especially. The detail he put into them was truly mind-blowing, especially in those days, when they didn't have cameras, but he did use the camera obscura, they reckon, predecessor of the modern camera. Anyway, this picture was faked maybe a couple of years back, and I'll tell you why I think that. The Heritage Trust lady told me it was missing from the wall about then, for several months, she said, while it was being cleaned. My bet is that it was removed not to be cleaned, but to be copied, and by an expert. I've actually restored and cleaned a Canaletto myself, and I noticed that this one wasn't quite right. Incredibly well painted – don't get me wrong – but not *quite* right. So to make sure I wasn't talking out of my arse, I borrowed that big Canaletto book from Adam, who took it out of the library, because we knew the actual Eggington Hall painting was featured in the book, didn't we Adam?'

I just nodded. When David was on a roll it was best to let him carry on.

'First, I took photos of it with my trusty Nikon and had Dunn's Photo Lab blow them up, and we went over it with my magnifying glass, and Adam will back me up here, little tiny details weren't quite the same, were they? The angle that a boatman's oar met the water, the boatman's hat, the hundreds of white ripples in the canal weren't in exactly the same places as the original – no one could get it *that* perfect, but then again, whoever faked it didn't expect me and Adam to go over it with a fine-toothed comb, did they?'

'So who do you think could have faked it, and why?' asked Andy.

'Hard to say, but it was a *very* good job. Professional forger stuff, he'd got the ageing canvas spot-on, and the frame was probably the original one. So I did a bit of digging. I asked my old mate, Henry Tibbatts, the former curator at The National Gallery in London, and he reckoned it might, just might, mind you, be a bloke named Marco Bellini, an Italian artist living in London who did time for forging Italian masters. One thing is certain, Chris, it wasn't you who did it; it would have looked more like a Lowry if that was the case!'

'Sarcastic twat!' grinned Chris, finishing his pint.

'So, here's our theory. Lord Billingham's stately home is a listed building, and he's not – I checked – allowed to sell off any stuff in the hall such as paintings, antiques and the like. That's probably why he's having trouble with getting hold of enough money to keep him in the lifestyle he's been accustomed to; Cessna planes, swanky cars and so on. So how do you raise a few quid? You pretend your Canaletto is going away to be "cleaned", and instead, you hand it to Marco Bellini or someone like him, and he copies it for you, and probably charges you a load of dosh, like, say fifty grand or more, which old Charles probably hasn't got spare. So he needs to organise a fence for the original Canaletto in advance. Step forward, Herr Grunstrasse, a slimy, obese, obnoxious bastard from Germany, who is known in the underworld to sell stolen famous paintings to private clients who hide their investments away in vaults. And he knows this area well. I actually encountered Grunstrasse years ago when he was buying a Monet from Lord Hickman of Stanmore castle,

109

near Stourbridge. It's a long story, but he turned up with his swivel-eyed pilot, Pierre van der Truck, a man who always carried a handgun, at Halfpenny Green aerodrome in a little four-seater, and took delivery of this Monet, which was owned by Lord Hickman's wife, who he was planning to leave, so he could live with his French mistress. He'd had the Monet faked, and put the forgery on the castle wall instead, so he could get some money from Grunstrasse to help fund his new life down under. That Monet would have fetched millions I reckon.'

'Bloody hell, David!' laughed Chris. 'Even I had no idea the art world was so corrupt. And who faked his Monet?'

'Erm, I'm afraid I did, but I can explain. He conned me into it by saying he needed a copy for the castle, good enough to fool the visitors, so he could put the real Monet in the vault for safe-keeping – something his insurance broker had suggested, as it was far too easy to steal a painting off a stately home wall.'

'Well, he was right there,' laughed Chris. 'Don't you think you were being just a tad naïve?'

'Well, I was a young art student at the time, so maybe, but in fairness, the excuse did sound plausible. Lord Hickman was later jailed for various crimes, and so was Grunstrasse, but that was ages ago. He'd probably be in his eighties now, if he's still with us, but people like him would have clients, often rich Americans apparently, who were after famous artworks to squirrel away as investments. Now imagine our Canaletto was worth fifteen million. You could sell it to Grunstrasse for five million, deduct your forger's fee of even a hundred grand, say, and *still* get four million, nine hundred thousand in your back pocket, tax free. And no one would be any the wiser, well, apart from me, obviously. The picture is still hanging on the stately home wall for the visitors to see, and everyone is happy! Now imagine if our sly old earl did that several times, with, say, his Titian, and his John Singer Sargent, and his Constable, and The Heritage Trust think they're all still on the walls, attracting visitors.'

We all took a fortifying slurp of alcohol to give this time to sink in.

'Jesus Christ!' said Andy. 'We need to interview the earl again, asap. Why don't we try it on with him? Tell him we know all about the phony painting and what he's up to, and see if he sings in return for a more lenient prison sentence. He was at least considerate enough to absolve his poor wife of any involvement in all this. He told us she had bugger all to do with anything, and he bullied her into lying about the Waldron portrait. I hear they have officially separated now too, which I for one am pleased about. She seems like a nice lady, unlike him.'

'He isn't a nice lady?' I asked with as straight a face as I could manage.

'You bloody know what I meant. And it's your round, I'm gagging here,' he fired back. 'Anyway, the only Constable and Sargent he'll be seeing any time soon is one of ours. Lord knows what a judge would charge him with. So far, potentially, we have; commissioning a fifteen-grand painting and not paying for it, causing an innocent man to go to jail, where he committed suicide, forging a Canaletto and maybe more artworks, and then selling the original or originals when he had no right to, bullying his wife into backing up his lies, not paying his £75 fine for parking without a ticket at Waitrose the other day, and whacking his missus across the face with a copy of Country Life.'

'Really?' I asked.

'Yes, he gave us that one for nothing. The whack in the face I meant, not the Waitrose fine. His secretary told me about that one. It was when his wife initially point-blank refused to back up his story about Michael Waldron being a nutter. He said he very much regretted getting physical, but it shocked her rather than hurt her.'

'I'd like to whack him with that Canaletto book from the library,' added David. 'That would hurt him as well as shock him. Art books are physically heavy as well as heavy going, trust me.'

We all stood up to leave, and shook hands. Chris and Andy thanked us both for our efforts and expertise, and said they intended to grill the earl again, this time with reference to faked paintings. They'd throw out a few names, such as Grunstrasse and Marco Bellini, just to gauge his reaction, and offer him a deal if he came clean about everything. As Chris was leaving The Plough, he called back to David.

'When I come to the next art class, can you show me how to forge paintings? It pays better than being a C.I.D. inspector, from what you're telling me.'

'It would be easier to teach Monet how to be a policeman!' David countered. A second later, a flying beermat hit him on the back of his neck. David acknowledged that he was a tad sarcastic, but there was no need for police brutality. The man was no better than the earl, assaulting folks with beermats! He had half a mind to report him to his superiors.

Chapter 16
A Surprise Visit

We had a quiet few days after that, and oh boy, did we need them. I played fetch the stick with Monty in my little rear garden, and took him for lots of walks. I like to get out into the countryside as often as I can, because I can't stand being sat at home watching daytime TV. There are umpteen adverts for a device called 'Revitive' that does something to your feet, featuring Eamonn Holmes and Ian Botham, who swear by them, apparently, endless repeats of 'Murder, She Wrote' and hundreds of bloody ads for worthy causes that drive me mad; the ads I mean, not the worthy causes. They want twenty quid a month off you to look after orphaned donkeys, thirty pounds and seven pence a month for starving kids in Africa – why the bizarre extra seven pence I'll never know, fifteen quid to help homeless people, and another huge chunk of your weekly wage for the R.S.P.C.A. If I contributed to every daytime TV charity ad, I'd be so broke that they'd start advertising for donations to help me next. I'm not decrying all these good causes, but nowadays they dictate exactly how much you have to send, rather than just ask you to give what you can afford, so surely, with this greedy new attitude, they are losing all those caring old pensioners who might have sent two pounds or whatever.

Meanwhile, David took Sooz to the Cotswolds and Stratford for days out, to make up for all the time he'd spent with me, on the trail of the lost Canaletto. I called round to his place to catch up, and he made me a cup of tea all by himself. Sooz had gone shopping with her mate

Mandy Stanier, Jon the estate agent's wife, to look for jeans, apparently. David said that his mate Chris, the police inspector, had popped by earlier to keep him up to speed. They'd taken the earl to the station in an absolutely foul mood, charged him, and he'd been released on bail. Typically, the court case was scheduled for some distant future date, so he'd been banned from disappearing to Italy or anywhere abroad, which, and I quote, 'pissed him off bigtime'. So the bloke was holed up in his Staffordshire pile, keeping a low profile and probably turning the refined air of the stately home royal blue. The man was beginning to make John Stonehouse look like a decent chap by comparison.

After David had passed all the police stuff on to me, he asked me about attending Michael's funeral, which was to be held at the Crem the following week. I of course said yes. He also mentioned that he'd been in touch with the solicitors, and he was just about to fill me in, when his doorbell chimed. He opened the door to a very pretty lady in her mid-thirties, with dark hair. He didn't need to ask who she was. He'd seen an oil painting of her. Suzannah Tavola, the Countess of Eggington, asked to speak to David Day, and having realised she already was, followed him into the barn's stylish living room, where I was sitting. We were introduced, she smiled a rather nervous smile, and sat down opposite me. I immediately noticed that she had a bruised eye.

'Excuse me,' she said. 'I walked into a door at the Hall the other day. I look a mess.'

David offered to make her a caffè latte from his swanky new machine, being as she was Italian. The bugger had never offered me one. I just got builders' tea.

'Please excuse the impromptu visit,' she said, rather nervously. 'I have a lot of explaining to do. I already spoke to your friend Chris, the policeman, and I told him I also wanted to see you two, so that you didn't think I was evil. He kindly told me where you lived, but only once he'd grilled me for an hour, which I know he has to do, so *non problemo*. I need to tell you my story, so I'm glad you're both here. I have been losing sleep.'

'Relax,' smiled David. 'We're nice people, we don't bite! Carry on.'

'I met Charles a few years ago, at an event. He was quite a lot older than me, but impressive and friendly. I suppose I fell for the English charm and the fact that he was a real-life earl from a stately home. I'm shallow like that!'

'Whereas you were just a beautiful young Italian woman who lived on an island in Stresa, next-door to a royal palace, where people such as Napoleon, Queen Victoria, and many famous writers stayed. I've been around the place. I've restored paintings there even. It is remarkable.'

'There's a difference between living in a palace and living next door to one, but I take your point,' she laughed. 'It wasn't quite a Cinderella meets Prince

116

Charming story, I admit, as my parents were quite wealthy too. I just fell for the man. For a while all was well, but he had a controlling side which gradually emerged. He asked a professional photographer to take some pictures of me some time back, but they were just slipped into a drawer and forgotten about, or so I thought. What he was actually planning was to give the shot he liked best to an artist he'd heard good reports about, to create an oil painting for my 35th birthday, as a surprise. It was to cost him £15,000 for three months' work, plus materials, he told me, but I was worth it! His words, not mine. Around that time, I noticed he was becoming more and more temperamental. I overheard a phone call he was making to an unknown man, and it sounded as if Charles was being threatened. From what I could make out, they were demanding a huge sum of money from him for something he'd been involved with, and he was telling this man he simply didn't have it. A few times, I saw some pretty shady-looking low-life types arrive at the hall, and he'd whisk them off somewhere to talk to them. Whenever I asked about them, he'd snap at me and say it was a private matter that he was dealing with. I reckon he'd done some kind of dodgy deal, and they were leaning on him. He asked if I could lend him some money a few times, and I did what I could, but when I queried why he was broke, he'd tell me that it was nothing to concern myself about. Things were being sorted out and all would be explained soon. I realise that running a stately home is tough. That's why The Heritage Trust and people like them take these places over, but this seemed – well, a bit sinister. After a while, it felt as if he'd only married me to get hold of *my* family's money, but he would never come clean about anything. Then this thing with the artist happened. He told me he'd commissioned it and could no longer afford it, so his plan was to eradicate all the evidence, take the picture to Italy, and swear blind the man was crazy. Who would you believe? A nutty old hippy artist who's banging on about a painting that doesn't exist, or a belted earl, a nobleman with a proud heritage; a pillar of the community. We had a blazing row, because it was just *so* wrong, what he was doing, and even worse, getting me to lie for him too, and then he went ballistic, grabbed me by the throat, and screamed, 'You will do as I fucking say, or we're both finished. And I *mean* finished, you stupid bitch. Dead!'

'Bloody hell!' David and I said in near perfect unison. She seemed a nice lady, and this was not what I wanted to hear. The man was obviously doing some dodgy dealing, and had got in far too deep. He'd stupidly commissioned a portrait he couldn't afford, or else, to give him the benefit of the doubt, he was maybe able to afford it when he commissioned the thing, but his circumstances changed dramatically not long afterwards. And it's just not on to tell the artist, 'Oh, I changed my mind', or 'I'm afraid I don't like it'. You can't just hand a picture back at that stage, after months of hard work, especially if there's nothing at all wrong with it, so instead, he does something infinitely worse and accuses the poor artist of being a fantasist loony! That way he gets to keep the portrait but not pay the bill. How low can you sink?

'I wanted to see you guys today,' she continued, her eyes welling with tears, 'because I didn't want you to think I was guilty of causing Mr Waldron's death. We had

118

such a nasty row after that, and I decided I didn't want any part of it, or Charles, any more. I couldn't live like that. I told him I wanted nothing of his whatsoever – I'd sign a solicitor's legal contract to that effect – and I was returning to live in Stresa, with my own money and my own house. I could not be part of all that subterfuge, and the terrible behaviour that had caused a man's death. I have a conscience even if he hasn't. He screamed and shouted at me, and told me to go away, so now I am. I've been holed up in one of the tied cottages since our row. I've had enough, and now it looks as if he'll end up in jail for what he did. I just hope whoever threatened him on the phone will disappear too. I just want a quiet life in Stresa.'

'I can fully understand that!' I said. Then she began to cry, so we sat each side of her and put our arms around her. We had no quarrel with this lady, just her bloody husband. The words, 'Be careful what you wish for' sprang to mind, and also the old Shakespeare one, 'All that glisters is not gold.' She was best advised to cut her ties, fly back to Italy and chalk it up to experience.

Chapter 17
The Funeral

Stourbridge Crematorium has a nice room that seats a fair few people, but I've been there when many mourners have had to stand outside under a canopy and listen to the loud-speakers instead. Michael's funeral wasn't one of those. We barely took up one half of a row of seats, to the right of the central aisle. It was me, David, Sooz, the countess, a solitary neighbour, Michael's distant relative, and that was it. Talk about sad. It was dismal. The vicar did his best with the sparse material he was given. Usually, a close relative or friend would supply interesting facts and anecdotes about the deceased, but in this case, there was nobody available, so he mentioned Michael's successful career as an artist, told us what a nice chap he was, principled and moral, someone who stood up for what he believed in, no matter what the personal price. David and I had scripted that bit for him. His neighbour had supplied a few extra bits and pieces too, such as Michael's love of Jimi Hendrix, The Beatles, Joni Mitchell, canal boats, fishing, country walks, watching Casablanca over and over again, and getting a bit emotional every time Bogart said, 'You played it for her, you can play it for me. If she can stand it, I can. Play it!'

The vicar also spoke about Michael's love for his wife, the only woman he'd ever been with, or ever wanted to be with. He added that her death had affected him so badly that he had begun to deteriorate mentally. The prison sentence they now knew he did not deserve added to that depression ten-fold, but even then, he would not give in when he knew he was right. This led to that sorry day when he realised that he'd had enough, and decided to end it all. Michael had not chosen any hymns, so that was a blessing. The thought of me, David, Sooz, the countess, a distant relative and his next-door neighbour struggling through an atonal rendition of 'Abide with Me' was too awful to contemplate. Instead, there were a couple of readings that he'd requested, namely sections of the two soliloquys from Hamlet, 'To be, or not to be' etcetera, etcetera, and 'O that this too too solid flesh would melt, thaw and resolve unto a dew, or that the Everlasting had not fixed his canon 'gainst self-slaughter. O God, God! How weary, stale, flat and unprofitable seem to me all the uses of this world'.

If you know your Shakespeare, these were extremely poignant, as both are spoken by another man who has had enough, and is also seriously contemplating suicide. Unlike Hamlet, however, Michael didn't just talk about it, he went ahead and did it. I looked either side of me to see how we all were, and the countess was crying her eyes out again. She knew that her husband's action had caused this innocent man's death, and that she had been complicit, albeit due to pressure from him. I saw David whisper in her ear, and whatever he said seemed to soothe her a little.

In between the two recitations, which, in fairness, the vicar did a very good job of, we heard 'Blue' by Joni Mitchell, and 'Eleanour Rigby' by the Beatles, which was so powerful, we were *all* reaching for our hankies. We thanked the vicar, dropped a fair bit of money in the tin on the way out, and said our goodbyes outside in the little pretty garden at the back. Michael was to join his wife for eternity. His reputation was restored. It meant a hell of a lot to us all. Mind you, that 'together again for eternity' bit is romantic nonsense, don't you think? Just stuff we say, to make it all sound lovely when it's not, like 'finally, you can rest in peace'. This is only my opinion of course, but Heaven is a bizarre concept, and fictional. It was created by human beings who couldn't face the thought of not existing any more, and I'm one of them, so I do understand the need for a fantasy world to make death appear slightly more palatable. The truth was that Michael and his poor wife no longer existed, they knew nothing about being next to each other, or about eternity. They weren't 'resting', they were dead. One claimed by cruel Mother Nature, and one destroyed by another person's greed and immorality.

Before we left, David introduced himself to Michael's distant relative, whose name was Carol Jennings. She admitted that she barely knew him; she was the second cousin of an aunt's brother's nephew's granny's sister-in-law; that sort of scenario. I glaze over when the connections get that complex. She felt guilty for even inheriting *anything* from the man, and told us she didn't deserve it. She was a very nice lady as it happens. David asked her if she had plans for the tatty old narrowboat, and she said she didn't. Michael also had a tatty old car and she didn't want that either. It was even worse than mine. David offered her £10,000 for the boat there and then, which was a tad too business-like for a funeral, I thought. She said, in response, 'It's yours, I wouldn't know what to do with it!' She'd already been left the proceeds from the sale of the flat, and a few other odds and ends, so she vowed to donate £5,000 of that to the Cobden Hospice, which was more than generous. She suggested that we all take a painting of our choice to remember Michael by, one for her, one for the neighbour, and one each for David and myself. Any paintings that were left after that, and there were at least twenty-odd that I counted, were to be sold at Fielding's Auction House in Stourbridge, and she also agreed to send the hospice a percentage of those sales too. Carol was, of course, also entitled to the £15,000 that the judge was going to screw out of the earl for the painting of Suzannah, and again, she would only accept a portion of it. She offered David and me the rest and we politely refused. I need the money, but not from that source. The lady was as generous as the earl had been mean. She thanked us for our efforts, and for defending Michael and proving him right, and all for no financial gain whatsoever. As David said afterwards, it was a desire to see justice done, and that beats financial gain hands down, every time. Corny, yes, but we meant it.

Carol also thanked Suzannah for siding with us and against her husband, and told her to take her portrait with her back to Stresa. The earl didn't want it, apparently. Surprise surprise! It was the best solution, because portraits don't fetch much money at auctions. They are so personal to the sitter or the immediate family, that no one else wants them. It would have been lucky to reach £500, David estimated, which was an insult to Michael, unless of course some ghoul bought it because of its notoriety; its back-story. Far better it resided in a house on Isola

Bella. No one blamed Suzannah for lying about the painting in the first place. We knew she was under considerable pressure from her husband, who, in fairness, was also under considerable pressure from some sinister characters, for reasons as yet unknown. That said, it was probably shady and illegal stuff that he'd become mixed up in, so my sympathy was, shall we say, scant.

I was a little surprised that there weren't any press people attending the funeral, but I suppose their focus was now on the earl, and all the shit they could dig up on him. I may be a minor journalist myself, but I have little respect for a lot of my peers, especially in the tabloids. They are ruthless, and would do almost anything to get a scoop, as we used to call it. I decided to write a touching and proper piece about Michael for the Stourbridge News, and anyone else who was interested, to put the story right after Michael had been ridiculed and wrongly judged in the nationals. Someone needed to tell his story, hence this book. I admit there is an uneasy alliance of comedy and tragedy within these pages, but that's life. Even Hamlet had its comedy moments. It helps the world go round in times of stress, I find.

All this set me thinking about what a diverse and weird set of people inhabit our world. We don't seem to have learnt a single thing in all those thousands of years, do we? There are people who would go to great lengths to save the life of a little kitten – vets, for example – and meanwhile, people have a great day out, shooting lions and tigers on Safari so they can pose beside the dead body with their rifle. Big macho men. They must be so proud!

Some folks are sent to prison for life for stabbing a person in the street, which is only right, and yet, Vladimir Putin is killing thousands of people for no reason, and instead of being in prison for life, he's the leader of a huge country. Kill one person, pay the price, kill several thousand, carry on! Some spend their days raising funds for starving kids in Africa while others broke into my elderly mother's house a few years ago and stole all the little bits of jewellery my late dad bought for her – stuff you cannot replace. She died not long after that. It was Jesus Christ who said, 'Do to others as you would have them do unto you.'

You could lose all the other pearls of wisdom that he uttered and just keep that one. It says it all, doesn't it?

Anyway, enough misery. Let's move on, eh?

Chapter 18
Confession is Good for the Soul

A few weeks back, Andy and Chris walked out of The Plough feeling that we had provided them with the right ammunition to do their job. It was Chris that rang David with the latest news, and asked him if he'd be good enough to also keep me up to speed with what they'd achieved in the interim period. I must admit, David had come up with a theory about the faked painting that made perfect sense. Who'd have thought that the art world, once just a haven for pure-minded folk who enjoyed the therapy, camaraderie and spiritualism of painting, drawing and sculpting, was now, on some fronts, just as toxic as a Columbian drug cartel? It was all about obscene amounts of money and investments, rather than the simple joy of looking at the beautiful thing hanging on one's wall. I wonder what poor old Vincent van Gogh would have made of it – a man who only ever sold one painting in his lifetime, and that to his brother. Fat lot of good all the current adulation has done him. It was far too late coming.

Anyway, the policemen thoroughly grilled the earl, and included all the stuff David had suggested to them, none of which was proven, remember, and the result was, he sang like a canary, and I don't mean that he made indecipherable tweety noises. He spilled the beans, coughed up, confessed. They pretended that they knew all about the Canaletto forgery, who painted it, who bought it, and who *he* sold it to. They explained that he would get a much-reduced sentence if he now co-operated, rather

126

than have them do more digging, so he did! Presumably, he knew the game was up and it now made more sense to tell all.

And here is the truly remarkable thing. Henry Tibbatts, ex-curator of The National Gallery, now retired, got it absolutely right about Marco Bellini, the prolific forger, and David also got it spot-on with the ageing art dealer, Herr Grunstrasse, who was still operating his seedy business at the age of eighty-five. Sadly, Grunstrasse wasn't opening up about who *he'd* then sold it to; not yet anyway. That was a work in progress. The painting was probably languishing in some U.S.A. millionaire's vault, in total darkness, longing to be looked at, pining for a well-lit gallery wall and appreciative visitors. What a fantastic waste of probably ten-or-so million quid. And what a tragedy that art was now nothing more than currency for people who probably didn't even appreciate its quality.

Chris and Andy had also got to the bottom of the sinister phone calls that Suzannah said she had overheard, and the shady, intimidating characters calling at the hall and demanding to see her husband. It transpires that Bellini was already in prison, having been caught by the London police not long back for forging a Gustav Klimt, and he had confided in his cell-mate, telling him about the Canaletto copy he'd just done for an earl, but hadn't yet been paid for. Apparently, the earl was, in turn, awaiting a payment from Grunstrasse, who was awaiting a payment from his client, who currently had other, more pressing issues to deal with, such as his high court trial for tax evasion. Sensing a new business opportunity, the cell-mate then contacted one of his gangster cronies on the outside, who decided to blackmail the earl about his little picture-faking scheme. At least these characters would no longer be a threat, Chris explained. It was hard to demand blackmail money from the earl if the police already knew he'd done it! Hopefully they'd crawl away now and try to extort cash from someone else.

'O, what a tangled web we weave, when first we practice to deceive' as Sir Walter Scott once wrote. What a nest of vipers, eh? It makes you proud to be honest, does it not?

All this owning up makes the earl sound contrite, but his confession was not made out of the goodness of his heart. It was purely and simply to get himself a lighter sentence. His behaviour was, as usual, self-serving. The one and only decent thing he'd done so far was to make it clear that his wife was not complicit in any of it. I, for one, would have hated to see such a nice lady dragged through all that.

Now the earl was in trouble. He was asset-rich but cash-poor, and that's not 'poor' as you or I would understand it, it's 'poor' as in, I might have to sell my aeroplane and not go to the Caribbean quite as often. He was reduced to faking pictures to make money, but not bothering to pay the forger. He was cheating The Heritage Trust, he'd commissioned an artist to create a portrait he had no intention of paying for; an artist who subsequently died because of his despicable actions, he was owed millions by a bent German art dealer, he'd been blackmailed by

128

gangsters, grilled by cops and abandoned by his wife, whom he'd whacked in the face with Country Life. Now *his* country life was dramatically falling apart. I almost felt sorry for him, but not quite.

Meanwhile, the police's biggest problem was knowing what to charge him with first. There was so much of it. They had done a magnificent job – not a sentence you hear about the police as often as you used to – but I have to say, these two were great, and credit where it is due. They explained to us that the court case could well be six months away, so it was best to put it to one side, and get on with our lives. We tried to, but it was difficult after all that excitement.

I met up with David for a coffee later that day. He was a bit bored because Sooz had gone to keep fit, and he couldn't understand why she still had to go twice a week. 'Surely,' he reasoned, 'she must be fit by now. She's been doing it for ages.'

He was glad the police-work had gone well, and couldn't wait for the trial to be concluded, so we could both get a sense of closure and move on. I was just leaving, an hour or so later, when he said, apropos of nothing, 'Adam, I was just thinking.'

Whenever he says something like that, I go a bit giddy.

'Do you think the Canaletto was the only one he had copied?'

129

Chapter 19
The Sentence

A lot of water had gone under the bridge since what happened in my last chapter. Six months' worth of water, to be precise, as the police correctly predicted. Nothing in legal circles is quick. I have realised this. I put a tiny little ex-council house on the market, that had been left to me by my late mother, and it sold within a week. This was eight months ago. It was sold to a man who had nothing to sell of his own; there was no chain, so it should have been simple, but no. I'm still waiting for the bloke's solicitors to complete the deal and hand over the money. Solicitors, in my humble opinion – not all of them, but a lot – are part sloth, part robot, and definitely a law unto themselves. You just can't hurry them. They remind me of that TV ad from years ago, 'Murray Mints, the too-good-to-hurry mints.' Solicitors, dear reader, are Murray Mints in human form. I can go out and buy a brand-new car in a day, but for some reason, a house takes months and months, and then, if the buyer decides that he doesn't want it any more, after eight months of fannying around, he can walk away scot-free, even though he's robbed you of eight months of your life, plus all those council tax payments, and heating bills. He's also robbed you of the opportunity to sell it to someone else. And, if all that wasn't bad enough, he's robbed you of the estate agent's fee, and your own solicitor's fee. Now who on earth deemed this to be a good way to do things? Apparently, the Scottish have a much better, fairer way of handling it.

I went off on one then, and I nearly lost the drift. I was talking about solicitors, and my point was going to be; all that house sale stuff is bad enough, but imagine that instead of a house, you're being held in prison for a year, awaiting trial, and then they find you not guilty. Who's going to give you that lost year back? God?

'Oh, sorry, Mr Twiddledick,' God would say, 'I was going to let you live to be seventy-two, but now I'll extend your life and let you live until your seventy-three to make up for it.'

At least the earl was freed on bail. I wonder if he was made to wear an ankle tag. I bet Tag Heuer make posh silver ones for the landed-gentry criminals. It would also serve as a reminder that they'd soon be doing *time*, come to think of it. See what I did there? Now, hang on, that's set me thinking. I reckon Rolex, Omega, Breitling and all that lot could make ankle tags for the rich and famous, as fashion statements when they wear shorts. Don't laugh, it could catch on. Ankle watches even. The next big thing! You read it here first, folks. I might contact the patents office when I've finished this paragraph.

I apologise, I'm going off on weird tangents today for some reason; I must reel myself in and concentrate. I have a tale to tell. In the last chapter, I left you in mid-air with David's line about there being potentially more fakes. It was a long shot, but the hall allowed him to check, just in case, and guess what – he searched the place from top to bottom and found another one. It was a dodgy John Singer Sargent oil painting from 1920, called 'The Rose Garden', which was hanging right next to the faked Canaletto. David asked some old colleagues from The National Gallery to examine it forensically, and they concluded that he was right. The oil paint was modern and made by Winsor & Newton circa 2003. It had been applied to a period canvas, after the former painting had been sanded back and covered over with white primer. The varnish was also modern, not Victorian. This meant that the earl had almost certainly dabbled in fakery well before the Bellini Canaletto. Chris and Andy were duly informed, and they put this to the beleaguered earl, who admitted to that one too, and then promised faithfully that that was the lot. Yeah! Okay. We'll believe you. They added this latest crime to his ever-growing list, and then popped to have a nice chat with Bellini and Grunstrasse again, no doubt singing 'A policeman's lot is not a happy one' from Gilbert and Sullivan's 'The Pirates of Penzance' as they drove along the M1 motorway.

Other than that extra bit of excitement, courtesy of Eggington Hall, our lives had settled back into calm, boring domesticity once more. I was knocking out the odd article for magazines and local papers, nothing worth a mention, sadly. David was always at Ashwood Marina, working on his forty-five-foot-long narrowboat, or else taking Sooz shopping for jeans, and drinking endless mugs of caffè latte at Marks & Spencer's café. Meanwhile, I was still spending my free days making a fuss of my new best friend, Monty, and taking him for loads of country walks. I was badly in need of female company, however – pining in fact – and I eventually plucked up the courage to ask Jan the librarian if she was free one of the nights, when I returned my Canaletto book, but as luck would have it, her colleague said she'd gone on holiday that week to Ireland to see her favourite folk band, 'The Fogeys', whoever they were, and I didn't ask either of her two colleagues instead, because the spray-tanned one with the Groucho Marx painted-on eyebrows seemed weighed down by her false eyelashes, and had a small dinghy where her lips should have been, whilst the other one looked like a sumo wrestler with pink hair, multiple tattoos and a nose-ring. I'm sure someone would find all that stimulating, but it wasn't for me. Instead, I watched crap films on Netflix and drank too much Shiraz. I don't know if you've ever trawled through the Netflix films, but you never know if they'll be brilliant entertainment or total rubbish. I watched a low-budget one the other night called 'Stop Lying to us, Mandible Raschenburger.' The synopsis was, 'Mandible is a Ukrainian pig farmer living in Utah, who discovers a bag containing $50,000 and a decomposing donkey in his shed. Then retired CIA agent, Deke Schritter, becomes involved, and things get complicated.'

It was the biggest pile of shite I've ever watched. Every American film nowadays must have a retired C.I.A. agent. It's mandatory. And a bloody car chase. And someone cautiously edging around a wall in a house that he's just gained entry to, his two arms stretched out in front of him, clutching a handgun. And there's always a baddie who's been knocked out by the lady of the house with a flower pot, and then you notice he's beginning to stir again and he's a few feet away from a discarded knife.

You probably want to know what happened to the Michael Waldron paintings that were found in his studio and his flat. Fielding's Auctioneers in Stourbridge took twenty-four of his artworks from us, and thanks to all the TV and newspaper coverage, there was an enormous amount of interest. The prices that they fetched exceeded all expectations, and the Cobden Hospice duly received just over eighty-thousand pounds from the sale, after the auction house commission and Carol's share, which was remarkable. Michael Waldron had become famous overnight, but, like so many other artists, he died before he could benefit from it. They always say that artists only get famous *after* they die, don't they, and it's mainly true, with a few exceptions. Strangely, this doesn't seem to apply to writers and musicians; it's just artists.

Interestingly, a lot of the ones who *do* succeed in getting famous in their lifetime become far *less* successful after they die. Take Beryl Cook, William Russell Flint, and David Shepherd, for example. Everyone collected their limited edition prints back in the day, and now you can't give them away. Ask the auction houses! If either of my kids wanted to become artists, I'd advise them against it, and suggest a career in football, where you earn the money early on, and then have ages left to spend it. A possible exception in the art world, though, might be David Hockney, who's made a packet in his lifetime and is still churning it out in his eighties, even if he is, shall we say, past his best nowadays. In my not-so-humble opinion, some folks also need to know when to stop. It'll be interesting to see if his popularity does continue after his eventual demise, though, or if it wanes quickly thereafter like the ones I mentioned earlier. It's probably best not to invest in any of his paintings, just in case. Not that you could ever afford one.

As to the earl, Chris and Andy explained to us that, because he'd confessed and was aiming to plead guilty in order to hopefully reduce his sentence, there would no longer be a trial. This was news to us. What I know about courts, the English legal system and all that, could be written on a postage stamp, and I'd still have room to jot down all I know about TikTok and Twitter. Even then, the stamp would probably have enough space left on it to list my favourite grime, rap and hip-hop artists, and remember, that's allowing for the portrait of King Charles and the price as well. As to the back of the stamp, I wouldn't need that side.

Thank God, then, that I had become quite friendly with Andy Moseley, who patiently explained to me the way courts work. I had no idea, for starters, that if a criminal chooses to fess up – see, I'm using trendy new expressions now – and plead guilty, there's no need for the jury, the prosecution and defence barristers, or the general public in the gallery. This upset David and me because we were looking forward to seeing all that Perry Mason stuff being acted out. Bewigged barristers, with their thumbs hooked into the top of their black gowns, demanding to know where the defendant was at 7.30pm on the night of the 25th. Lawyers saying 'M'Lud' when addressing the snooty judge, with his half-moon spectacles perched on the edge of his beak. One of them shouting 'Objection, Your Honour,' and the judge saying 'Sustained!', or maybe 'Overruled!'. Watching nervous witnesses take the stand and swearing on the Holy Bible. The spokesperson for the jury, telling us that they had reached a unanimous verdict. We had been denied all of this. We wanted our day in court! Andy also explained something to me about Michael's theft of the Canaletto, and guess what? It wasn't theft. He showed me a law book that explained, in mind-numbing detail, the difference between stealing something and hiding it away, as Michael had done. There were the usual ten million sub-clauses about the precise nature of the act, all of which made a difference to the possible punishment, or lack of it. I won't bore the pants off you with all that, but suffice it to say that Michael's version, i.e., hiding an item as a protest against wrongdoing by the earl, within the house where it belonged anyway, and his clear intention to eventually reveal its whereabouts, as illustrated by the cryptic clues he left us, added up to a big fat 'no crime committed' conclusion. So he should never have gone to jail.

On the other hand, the earl's commissioning of two faked masterpieces, the sales of both original paintings to a crooked art dealer for millions of pounds, plus his non-payment of a £15,000 debt for no good reason, and his subsequent act of perverting the course of justice by telling malicious lies that caused an innocent man to be jailed – well, all that was adding up to a pretty serious amount of jail-time. The judge took into consideration his guilty plea, the fact that he was desperate and not in his right mind because he was in debt and being blackmailed, plus his 'genuine' remorse about what he'd done to his wife and Michael Waldron, and then handed him a sentence of seven years in prison. Andy reckoned he'd do a year in a 'proper' prison, followed by a stretch in a cushy open prison, and he'd probably only do half of his sentence if he behaved, and then go back to his stately home or wherever.

As soon as this was relayed to us, we rang Suzannah in Stresa to give her the news. That resulted in more tears, as we expected, but we assured her that she had done the right thing and was better off without him. She agreed, and even hinted that a brand-new romance was in the offing.

Chapter 20
The Artist is Restored

'Did you know that Jerome K. Jerome used to live in Stourbridge?' David asked.

'No I didn't,' I replied, 'I thought he was from Walsall.'

'He was, but when he was little, his dad had a place in Worcester Street, near the park, I think. Now *he* was a comedy writer!'

'He certainly was,' I agreed. 'One of my heroes, comedy-wise. "Three Men in a Boat, and a dog called Montmorency," a comedy classic!'

'And did you cotton on that this, my partner in crime, is "Four Friends in a Boat, and a dog called Monty"?

David, Sooz, Jan the Librarian, me and my beloved new dog, Monty, were on board 'The Artist' for her maiden voyage, from Ashwood Marina, down the canal to Stourport and then onto the mighty River Severn towards Worcester. 'The Artist' looked magnificent, I must admit. She had been a labour of love for David. He'd had the boat in dry dock, completely stripped down, repaired and repainted in the traditional reds, yellows and greens, with a nice stripy tiller. He'd done all the signwriting himself, as you'd expect, and of course, as promised, he'd kept the original name. He had also added a sentence underneath the boat's name that said "Dedicated to Michael Waldron, Artist". All of the interior had been completely refurbished, and new tartan upholstery added. It was wonderful; he'd done a lovely job of it, as you'd expect. Outside, we were celebrating in style. Sooz and David had been given a huge bottle of Prosecco for Christmas by their son, Jamie, and his girlfriend, Ellie, but had not yet opened it. Sooz was worried that two people would find it too much to finish off in one night, and feared it would go flat. Either that or they'd somehow manage to finish it off, and then *they'd* go flat, so she had waited for a suitable occasion to pop the cork, and this was it. She was playing waitress, and topping up everyone's glasses, except for David's, and of course, Monty's. David had a small glass to show willing, and then abstained. He was skippering the vessel, and didn't want to be done for being drunk and disorderly in charge of a narrowboat. He said he'd make up for it at The Plough, when he got home, if they ever did. He insisted that he didn't drink until the sun had gone over the yardarm, but when I questioned him about what a yardarm was, he didn't have the faintest idea. When he was a young man at art college, his mate, Dylan, had been on a narrowboat trip to celebrate the end of term – it was a huge floating bar that travelled from Wolverhampton, where the college was, to Kinver, and he was, by the time he arrived in Kinver, frankly, legless. He popped off the boat to relieve himself against a tree, as men tend to do (why *do* we need something to pee against?), and then walked straight into the lock and nearly drowned, because his cowboy boots filled up with water and weighed him down. He somehow got out alive, and picked up his bike from a friend's house, to cycle home to Stourbridge. Then he drove it straight into a couple's privet hedge and got done for drinking and cycling by a copper on the beat who witnessed the incident. Yes, this was back in 1974, when we still had them – coppers on the beat I meant, not bikes, obviously.

Before we set off on our adventure, I had received a postcard from Suzannah Tavola, so I brought it with me to show everyone. It said:

Ciao bello! I am back living in Stresa full-time, as you know, and life is good. My life was in turmoil at Eggington Hall, with a man I thought I knew, but didn't. Now I have a new love in my life, a fellow Italian, called Giovanni, who is lovely and kind. Not well off, but I don't care. He has met you two, by the way, so he says hello. Yes, he's one of the decorators. The one you conned into handing over my portrait! It is now back in the dining room, and I treasure it. Grazie mille. If you are ever here again, you can stay at the house, gratis. Any time. Plenty of room. I mean it, love Suzannah. Xxx

We had a great afternoon on that boat. The Severn was twinkling in the sunshine, just like Lake Maggiore was that weekend when we were there. Swans, Canada geese and hundreds of mallard ducks were paddling about, just like they were in Stratford, enjoying the nice weather. The ducks all seemed to have seven or eight cute little babies in tow, all trying to keep up with their parents. Occasionally, one would zoom off on its own, and the daddy duck would have to chase after it and round it up. There's always one unruly kid in every family isn't there?

Sooz, the queen of the daft question, poured herself yet another Prosecco and asked, apropos of nothing, if Canada geese chose their mates according to their temperament, or their intelligence.

'Why do you ask?' said Jan the Librarian, puzzled.

'Well, it can't be their looks, can it? They all look identical!'

It was a fair point, I thought. Her thoughts turned to swans now.

'I don't trust them,' she informed us, as two came close to the boat and started hissing at Monty. 'Their eyebrows meet in the middle. They've got mono-brows. They look like that Frida Kahlo artist woman.'

At that point, we sailed through a huge cloud of gnats that we didn't see coming, a constant problem on canals and rivers, and we were spitting them out, blowing our noses, cleaning out our ears and shaking them out of our hair for the next ten minutes. At least twenty of the little bastards were swimming in my Prosecco, and Monty, who looked lovely in his little lifejacket, by the way, was barking at them and swishing his ears about.

'Have gnats got lungs?' Sooz asked, as soon as we had cleared the gnat-cloud, and she had cleared her throat.

'How the hell would I know?' asked David. 'I'm not David Attenborough, I'm David Day. Why on earth do you want to know?'

'Just wondered,' she replied, flicking the last one out of her drink. 'What about a brain, and a heart?'

It was another good question. Sooz had a habit of asking these questions that no one else had ever thought about. If gnats had a heart, it would be absolutely tiny. And imagine having a brain that small, to fit in a gnat's head. And then it set me thinking about what gnats thought about. And how much food they'd need to fill their little stomachs. Sooz, I must admit, was good company and very funny in a droll kind of way, but, according to David at any rate, she had the lowest boredom threshold he had ever encountered. A slightly mundane conversationalist would cause her to completely glaze over in seconds, or maybe even wander off, and this could be mentally wander off, or wander off in the physical sense – suddenly go and sit somewhere else. Sometimes he would ask her something and she wouldn't even respond. He told me about a time when she complained that her large frying pan was scratched to pieces and past its sell-by date, hence she needed another one, so being the dutiful husband, he drove her to Marks & Spencer to buy one. After what he reckons was around thirty seconds spent looking at them, she declared that she was too bored to continue, and headed for the café. They say that opposites attract, and so it was with those pair. She was the yin to his yang, whatever that means.

We were approaching a lovely picturesque spot called Holt Fleet now, and this seemed to inspire David, who suddenly began singing 'A Life on the Ocean Wave.' However, he only knew the first line of the song, and so did we, so the rest was just 'and a tiddly tiddly tee!' This lasted some way down the river, causing passing boaters and the odd angler to stare at us in disbelief. Then it was Jan the Librarian's turn to contribute to the madness.

'Did you know that a parrot was arrested recently by Brazilian police, for acting as a lookout for a criminal gang?'

'You can't arrest a parrot,' a slightly slurred Sooz replied.

'Well, they did!' Jan insisted. 'It was in the Daily Mail!'

I had a funny feeling that the Prosecco was doing its job. We were all giggling like idiots now. Anything and everything seemed to make us laugh. David told us about his mobile phone messages, which he'd often type in a hurry and not check before sending them. Recently, he'd meant to type 'semi-skimmed milk' and actually wrote 'semi-skilled milk'. On realising his mistake, he resent the text to Sooz and this time wrote 'semi-stiffed monk'. A few weeks after that, he sent a text to a lady who'd asked him to give a talk to a retirement group in Dudley. She said he could either be paid a set fee, or if he preferred, they could charge two-pounds-fifty per head on the night. He wrote back, 'Let's take a gamble on the head-count.'

Unfortunately, he'd missed out the letter 'o' in the final word. He was still haunted by that one.

We moored the boat on a beautiful stretch of river. It was soon going to be time to return to the marina, before it got dark. These canal boats are lovely, but they don't travel very fast. In fact, you can walk quicker. Sooz had prepared a buffet, down in the boat's main cabin, and I, for one, was starving. Michael Waldron had never been given a wake, so this was our version of it. David allowed himself half a glass more Prosecco and addressed us.

'My friends, thank you for coming today. La vendetta è un piatto que va servito freddo, as they say in Italy, so today, it is fitting that we have a buffet served cold for you. Sadly, nothing will bring him back, but at least justice has finally been done. To Michael!'

We raised our glasses and called out, 'To Michael.' We ate, drank and were merry. Sooz had also prepared a nice little dish of food for Monty, so he didn't feel left out. Then, an hour or so later, stomachs full, we went back up on deck, and we set off back towards Stourport, and believe it or believe it not, we sailed off into a glorious sunset.

THE END

Where are they now?

Friedrich Grunstrasse died of a heart attack whilst serving his sentence in a German prison. He was eating his lunch at the time.

Marco Bellini is currently halfway through his sentence at a London prison. He gives painting lessons to the artistically-inclined inmates every Wednesday.

Lord Charles Billingham is now in an open prison in Shropshire. He is writing his autobiography and appears to be contrite and remorseful, according to the governor anyway.

The Cobden Hospice named a new wing of their premises after Michael Waldron. It's called the Michael Waldron Wing.

Suzannah Tavola is now Suzannah Gallani. Her beautiful new daughter was christened Lily.

Andy and Chris are still senior police officers.

David and Sooz are probably on their narrowboat somewhere. Either that or they're at Marks & Spencer's café, Kidderminster. Sooz is seeking professional help for her jeans addiction.

Jon Stanier made his first ever century at the age of fifty-six. His final six hit Hoss Cartwright on the brow, but he was not seriously hurt. Jon has now been given the nick-name 'Brainer' by his team-mates.

Monty and I are still together, but sadly, Jan the Librarian married a Fogey and moved to Ireland.

The Eggington Hall Canaletto and 'The Rose Garden' by John Singer Sargent have not yet been found.

145

Front cover image

Portrait of the author's daughter, Laura,
pretending to be Countess Suzannah Tavola,
taken by Geoff Tristram

She still hasn't paid me for it.

Comedy and tragedy don't, at first glance, appear to be good bedfellows, but I would argue that they are. Humour can rescue you when you are at the end of your tether. Shakespeare knew that, and who would argue with *him*? It is the paracetamol for your headache; the anaesthetic for your life-saving operation. It is the difference between suicide and sleeping on it till tomorrow, for tomorrow is another day. If you can find humour in your darkest hour, it can give you hope.

There is a huge difference between laughing *at* someone in distress, and laughing *with* them to lift their spirits. It is not disrespectful, or at least, my comedy hopefully isn't. Comedy is optimism. It can promise a bright new dawn, no matter how awful the night has been.

The inspiration for this story was something that actually happened to me, though thankfully, in my case, it was far less traumatic or severe than it was for poor Michael. Nevertheless, it upset me greatly at the time, and will stay with me forever, especially as it was all about my final commission before I retired. Not a great way to end a fantastic career, but this book was cathartic. My stark choice was either legal action, which would have been unpleasant (though I would have won without a shadow of a doubt), or else to write this book. There is nothing litigious in it whatsoever. The plot is completely different, the characters are all invented, as are their names. My time working in Italy taught me a sentence, which I found could be used in a therapeutic way as well as a vicious way. It was 'La vendetta è un piatto que va servito freddo' which translates as 'Revenge is a dish best served cold.' Let the dust settle, I was advised, and think carefully about your response, which is what I have done.

Nothing is wasted in life. A situation that hurts at the time will eventually become a funny anecdote, a bit like when I accidentally electrocuted myself in the testicles trying to photograph a cow, as artist's reference for a job I was doing. I didn't realise it was an electric fence. It hurt so much that I fell backwards down a muddy bank into a quagmire of liquid cow manure, whilst wearing my best suit. I can't remember being overly amused at the time, come to think of it, but now, thirty years later, I can't remember that incident without laughing my head off, and laughter, as they say, is the best medicine.

Books in the David Day series:

A NASTY BUMP ON THE HEAD

Eleven-year-old David Day finds the curmudgeonly toy-shop owner, Miss Kettle, murdered in her shop. He duly informs Scotland Yard, only to bump into her in Tenbury Wells the following week.

MONET TROUBLE

First-year art student David Day is persuaded to forge a Monet painting by the mysterious Lord Hickman, but unknown to either of them, several other artists have the same idea.

VINCENT GOUGH'S VAN

An art-college murder-mystery of Shakespearian proportions, littered with psychic sewing teachers, psychotic students, and lesbian assassins.

THE CURSE OF TUTTON COMMON

David sets about trying to improve Britain's worst museum, and assisted by a cat named Hitlerina, he discovers an ancient Egyptian tomb in South Staffordshire.

PAINTING BY NUMBERS

Thirty-year-old David is having a mid-life crisis, made worse by the fact that his art studio has exploded, and the ninety-year-old 'Paint by Numbers' enthusiast he has befriended is not what he seems.

STEALING THE ASHES

Forty-year-old David Day overhears two Australian cricketers plotting to steal the Ashes, and, ably hampered by his mate Laz, he tries his best to thwart their plans.

THE HUNT FOR GRANDDAD'S HEAD

The prequel to Nasty Bump! Daleks have invaded Brierley Bank, but David harnesses their power to see off the neighbourhood bully.

DAVID'S MICHELANGELO

David's best mate, Laz, opens a restaurant in an old chapel and asks David to decorate the ceiling with copies of Michelangelo's artwork. Then, during a visit to the Sistine Chapel in Rome, David makes an earth-shattering discovery.

THE TEA BAG MURDERS

Semi- retired and bored, David needs a project. He spots an article in the Daily Mail about a serial killer who stuffs tea bags into his victims' mouths, so he asks a member of his monthly art class, C.I.D. Inspector Chris Smith, if he can be of assistance, as he has a theory about the killer's bizarre trademark.

***

Books in the Adam Eve series:

THE CURIOUS TALE OF THE MISSING HOOF

Writer Adam Eve hires a pantomime-horse costume, but forfeits his deposit when he loses one of the hooves. His obsessive efforts to locate it create mayhem!

MR MAORI GOES HOME

Adam Eve's hell-raising uncle has died and left him a substantial amount of money – on the condition that he returns a rare Māori carving to New Zealand.

LOSING THE PLOT

Adam writes a sure-fire best-selling novel, only to lose his only copy of it. Can he find his stolen laptop and bring the thief to justice?

A REMARKABLE CHAIN OF EVENTS

Adam joins forces with David Day to discover a Shakespearean masterpiece that rocks the world.

A LIFETIME SPENT WATCHING PAINT DRY

The illustrated autobiography. Be warned, it'll make you laugh, and it'll make you cry.

*Geoff has also written a stand-alone comedy, **The Last Cricket Tour.**

He sent this and '**Stealing the Ashes**' to Guy Lavender, the Chief Executive of Lord's Cricket Ground in London, and had one of the nicest, most flattering replies he's ever had. What a lovely man!

And if you need children's picture books,

Welcome to the Curious Zoo

A collection of nonsense poetry and lovely illustrations of crazy, made-up animals that your child will love.

You may also like the companion books, written by David Tristram and illustrated by Geoff Tristram

The Giant Panteater and other Curious Creatures
and
Poetry in my Ocean

All available from Geoff at Drawing Room Press, email below.

As well as his long list of comedies, Geoff has written the splendid, limited edition, illustrated coffee-table book,

JB's: The Story of Dudley's Legendary Live Music Venue

which charts the rise and eventual sad demise of England's longest-running rock club – a venue which played host to many of the biggest bands in the world, before they became famous.

Sadly, all 3,000 of the limited-edition copies have now been sold to JB's fans worldwide, so look out for a rare second-hand copy on eBay and snap it up! It's becoming a collector's item.

THE VENDETTA CÀFÉ

A black comedy set in a café in Stratford-upon-Avon. The lives of the various customers become intertwined, as the plot thickens in a very Agatha Christie kind of way, and nothing is as it seems. Expect subterfuge, lies, twists and turns, and a truly explosive ending!

And, a book which also features some of Geoff's brilliant cartoons.

So, yeah!
(500 Things that irritate the hell out of me)

Geoff lets rip with a list of things that drive him mad, from mispronounced words, woke students, bad grammar, hypocrisy, fashion, TV programmes, bad music, graffiti, Americans, pets, advertisements, and much, much more!

A book to divide the nation, no less, all delivered with his tongue firmly in his cheek.

For more information, or to order a signed copy

email gt@geofftristram.co.uk

Website: www.geofftristram.co.uk